Runestruck

Runestruck

By **Calvin Trillin**

Little, Brown and Company
Boston, Toronto

FIRST EDITION

T02/77

Library of Congress Cataloging in Publication Data

Trillin, Calvin.
  Runestruck

  I. Title.
PZ4.T83Be   [PS3570.R5]   813'.5'4   76-45610
ISBN 0-316-85275-9

Designed by Christine Benders

*Published simultaneously in Canada
by Little, Brown & Company (Canada) Limited*

PRINTED IN THE UNITED STATES OF AMERICA

To Josie Davis

Columbus sailed the ocean blue
In fourteen hundred and ninety-two.
— *American children's chant*

Go back where you came from!
— *American grown-ups' chant*

Runestruck

D UANE MINNICK WAS SINGING a country-and-western song of his own composition — "I Ain't Bowlin' in Your Bowlin' League No More." In the nineteen years he had been alive, Duane had never ventured more than forty miles from Berryville, a town on the southern coast of Maine, but spiritually he was a prisoner of Nashville. When he was at home, Duane pawed at an electric guitar, producing sounds that more or less matched the beat, if not the precise tone, of his singing. Away from home, he simulated guitar sounds while thwacking away on whatever straight implement was at hand — in this case, a rake with which he was supposedly digging clams. "You bowled a strike when it came to me," he sang, "But now we're split and I can see / You used me as a spare /

3

Though it really wasn't fair / Then you told me as you left me at the door — thwack, thwack — That I ain't bowlin' in your bowlin' league no more."

"Awful!" Clifford Bates shouted from twenty yards away, where he was actually using his rake to dig clams. "That's just awful, Duane. Awful. That is one awful song." Clifford Bates had heard more of Duane's songs than anybody else. They worked at Earl's Texaco together and went clamming together and tinkered with their cars together and occasionally even accompanied each other on visits to Myrna McDonald, who, it had often been said in Berryville High School, "would do anything to anybody for an orange soda." Clifford's response to Duane's songs was consistent in that he had never heard one he liked. The closest Clifford had ever come to encouraging Duane was to admit, in an uncharacteristically charitable moment, that Duane theoretically could have composed a good song at one time or another without anybody's having known it, since his voice would make even a lovely song sound awful. Art Norton, the editor of the Berryville *Advance,* who had been an involuntary member of Duane's audience several times while buying gas at Earl's Texaco, had once referred to Duane's voice as "the only pure example of the nasal monotone in southern Maine."

Duane had taken no offense at Clifford's response to the bowling league song. He had inoculated himself against criticism by having read in a country-music magazine that Johnny Cash — or perhaps it was Merle Haggard — had written seventy-three songs before coming up with one that anybody would publish. "Didn't you really like that one, Clifford?" he said.

"Why don't you unplug that guitar and try to get some clams, Duane," Clifford said. They had just come to the end of a point of land called Sandy Thumb and Duane was nearing a boulder that had been described to him by a customer at Earl's Texaco as practically a clam-magnet. It was a warm day in June, but the water in Berryville Harbor was still frigid; both boys walked as if in slow motion to guard against water sloshing over the top of their clamming boots.

"You didn't like that — really?" Duane said, as he finally reached the boulder and started poking around for clams. "How do you think it compared to the one I wrote last week — 'I'm Just a Loaner While You Wait for the Two-Door Hardtop of Your Dreams'?"

"Well, I'll tell you," Clifford said. "Before this bowling song, I used to think that two-door hardtop song was the worst song that anyone could ever write. Now, I'm not so sure."

Just the mention of the two-door hardtop song, even a less than enthusiastic mention, brought the rake around to electric-guitar position in Duane's hands, and he began to sing: "You went out and bought you some automobile. / I was out of your heart when you closed the deal — thwack, thwack — You used to be here, but right now you're there. / You done left me for chrome and factory air."

Clifford, groping for a response adequate to the two-door hardtop song, picked up a flat rock and skipped it across the water with a bounce that drenched Duane. As Duane reached down to find a rock that seemed large enough to use for retaliation, Clifford stepped nimbly behind another huge boulder. There was a long silence.

"Hey, Clifford," Duane finally shouted.

"What is it, Duane?" Clifford said, remaining behind the protection of the boulder.

"I got me a real strange rock here, Clifford."

"A big rock?"

"Yeah."

"Kind of round?"

"Yeah, yeah," Duane said. "Kind of round."

"That's your head, Duane."

"C'mon, Clifford, I'm not shittin' you," Duane said. "It's got some weird writing on it."

"Does the first word look like a 'C,' Duane?"

"I can't really read it very good," Duane said, rubbing at the rock to clear the mud away.

"Kind of C-looking, is that what it's like?" Clifford shouted from behind the boulder.

"Yeah, Clifford. I guess it does look sort of like a 'C.' "

"Well, that's cause it says 'Cram This up Your Keister,' " Clifford said, and he started cackling. Listening to Duane's songs was often excruciating, but Clifford Bates thought it was a small price to pay to be in the company of someone who could be suckered twice in a row with ease. He waited for Duane's response. He expected some country song, something like "Our Love Is on the Rocks but That Stone on Your Finger Is Mine." There was only silence. Cautiously, Clifford crept out from behind the boulder. Duane was standing in a foot of water, staring at the stone he held in his hand.

"Let me see that goddamned rock, Duane," Clifford said, after making certain he wasn't walking into a trap. He examined the stone — an almost white oblong stone about six inches long. There was definitely some sort of writing on it, but writing that used letters Clifford had never seen before. "Jesus, that *is* weird," he said. "Maybe it's Indian or something, and we can sell it to the summer people. Summer people are apeshit for Indians."

"I told you it was a real weird rock, Clifford," Duane said. "Real weird."

"Of course, the summer people might just want to know whose land we crossed to find it and what we were doing there and don't we have any respect for other people's property, and all that," Clifford said. As far as he knew, nobody who lived around Berryville owned Sandy Thumb, but the land just across the cove from it belonged to Gerald Baker Manley, a noted civil liberties lawyer from Boston, who was known in Berryville mainly for having enclosed the fourteen acres surrounding his summer house with an electrified fence. In an escapade that they considered their greatest triumph, Clifford and Duane had managed to pole-vault the fence and replace all of Manley's No Trespassing signs with signs that faced his house instead of the fence and said "Up Yours."

"It's a real weird rock, all right," Duane said.

"Maybe we should take it to old Brewster up at the library," Clifford said. "He's always digging up arrowheads and Coke bottles and all."

Duane made no reply. He was staring at the stone.

"Duane?" Clifford said. Duane continued to stare at the stone silently.

"I've got it!" Duane finally said. "I've got it, Clifford!"

"You mean you can read that weird writing?" Clifford said, although he knew very well that Duane had experienced difficulties at times reading ordinary English.

"No, no. I got the song," Duane said. He began to sing, using the stone as an oversized pick for playing his rake. "The rocky road of love cracked the axle of my heart — thwack, thwack — This broken heart of mine just ain't a-gonna start."

Clifford reached over and took the stone from Duane's hand. "Awful, Duane," he said. "That one is just awful."

Lawrence I. DiCarlo, the mayor of Berryville, heard of Duane Minnick's discovery the following morning while drinking the first of the eight or ten cups of coffee he customarily consumed every day at the Yankee Cafe, on Main Street. DiCarlo never had more than one cup of coffee at a sitting. In fact, he rarely managed a posture at the Yankee Cafe that could precisely be called sitting. He always seemed in such a hurry to be on his way that he drank his coffee while in a sort of half-crouch, his chair pushed back from the table and one foot already pointed toward the door. Larry DiCarlo stayed on the move. He had an office at City Hall and an office at his own business — Lawrence I. DiCarlo, General Contracting — but his visits to either office were made at the pace of a meter-reader who had fallen way behind. If a telephone call caught him at a desk, he tended to deal with it while standing, reaching for a pile of mail that he could sort on the way out. He undoubtedly spent more time seated in his bright red pickup truck — guiding it between his mayoral office and the Yankee Cafe and his contracting office and the site of whatever construction he was overseeing and back to the Yankee Cafe — than he did seated anywhere else, and some people in Berryville were in the habit of referring to the pickup as City Hall. DiCarlo was a short, voluble man whose reaction at one heated City Council meeting to being called "excitable" by a political opponent had been to shout "That's a goddamned lie!" and bring the mayor's gavel down hard enough to shatter its stem beyond repair.

It was only seven forty-five — DiCarlo was the only

person in the Yankee Cafe except the proprietor, Mike Derounian — but he already seemed to be in a hurry to leave.

"I hear Duane Minnick found some sort of valuable rock or stone or something out at Sandy Thumb," Mike Derounian said, as DiCarlo started sipping rapidly at his coffee.

"Duane Minnick?" the mayor said. "Which one's Duane Minnick?"

"Tom Minnick's boy," Derounian said.

"The one in the Army that hit his sergeant?"

"No," Derounian said. "The younger one. The one that works at Earl's Texaco — the one who's always singing all those hick songs that even my kid can't stand to listen to."

"The one that works at Earl's Texaco!" the mayor said, raising his voice a bit. "The one that works at Earl's Texaco couldn't find his own ding-dong if you told him to look between his legs."

"Well, I guess this rock or whatever is pretty important, all right," Derounian said.

"I don't know what that Minnick kid found," Mayor DiCarlo said. "But if he was the one that found it I can tell you it's not worth a nickel retail."

"Sam Brewster says it's old as hell, from what I hear," Derounian said.

"Sam Brewster!" the mayor said, loudly. "Sam Brewster thinks that just about anything that doesn't have the warranty printed right on it is an antique from the goddamned Middle Ages. You pick up any rock you want out of the creek and show it to Sam Brewster and Sam Brewster will look squinty-eyed at it and tell you that rock was undoubtedly an arrowhead that once had to be removed from the ass-end of the chief of the Ogunquit Nation. You're talking to a man now who was there when they showed Sam Brewster that thing someone found near the dump and Sam said he thought it might be an ancient Indian kettle for cooking up entrails or something and it turned out to be one of those hibachis some summer person had ordered from Abercrombie and goddamned Fitch."

"Well, I'm getting this secondhand, Larry, but I hear Sam says it's maybe a thousand years old, left by some Swedes or something."

"If Sam says a thousand, that means two hundred," DiCarlo said. "I always divide everything he says by five. If he tells me there used to be twenty Indian tribes around here, I figure maybe four. Even when he just says hello, I divide by at least three."

Derounian left to give menus to two more customers who had just come in. When he returned, he brought up the subject of the Yankee Cafe's roof, which had leaked intermittently since Lawrence I. DiCarlo, General Contractor, had renovated the building two years before.

Mention of the roof brought the mayor the rest of the way out of his chair. He finished his coffee standing up, facing the door. "I thought I sent someone over to fix that," DiCarlo said, sounding somewhat offended that somebody would bring up such a subject to the mayor of the city practically in his own office — or at least in a place he visited so often during the day that people who had to see him on city business were accustomed to waiting in one of the Yankee Cafe's booths rather than on the wooden benches of City Hall.

"Nobody ever came, Larry," Derounian said. "It's been two weeks since you told me someone was coming."

"Jesus, we haven't had a big rain all month," DiCarlo said, starting toward the door. "It's not like it's a big emergency or anything." The subject of roofs irritated the mayor. He had been fairly successful in the contracting business, but he couldn't seem to do roofs. Sooner or later, there were always complaints about leaks. The Main Street businessmen who gathered for coffee at the Yankee Cafe delighted in the subject of roofs. "You hear about a lot of towns where the mayor allows leaks from the administration," Art Norton of the *Advance* had once said. "We just happen to have the only mayor who allows leaks from the roof." It often seemed to DiCarlo that if the coffee-drinkers in the Yankee Cafe didn't have potholes to talk about — potholes that had not been repaired by the city — they would be able to talk about nothing but leaks in his presence. "I'll have somebody around — don't worry about it," DiCarlo said to Derounian, as he rushed off toward the door. "For Christ sake, Mike, can't you see I'm in a hurry?"

When, on the previous afternoon, Duane Minnick and Clifford Bates had arrived at the Berryville Free Library, dripping water from their clamming boots on the vestibule floor, Sam Brewster was downstairs in the museum, engaged in one of his periodic arguments with Millicent Duffrin. Brewster's engagement in an argument with Millicent Duffrin was actually rather limited, being confined to shaking his head slowly now and then and occasionally mumbling, "I'm sure sorry you feel that way, Milly." Millicent Duffrin, a retired schoolteacher, was the president of the Berryville Historical Society — an organization that she ran with such single-minded attention to proving the distinction of her own family that Art Norton often referred to it as the Berryville Duffrinical Society. She made regular visits to the library, ostensibly to do historical research but actually to accost Sam Brewster and accuse him of using his position to suppress evidence that might tend to prove, once and for all, that the Duffrins had been in Berryville long before the Brewsters wandered in, and were therefore the oldest family in town.

"And these displays are a disgrace, Samuel," Milly

Duffrin was saying. "A bunch of old broken up pots and Indian knickknacks. For all the mention seen of Josiah Duffrin, who happened to have cleared the forty acres this town was founded on, he might as well have arrived in nineteen-twenty with a load of French-Canadian mill-hands. I think you should bear in mind that the ancestors of the taxpayers who count in this town were people like Josiah Duffrin and not a bunch of savages."

Sam Brewster happened to be completely innocent of using his position to promote his own ancestors, although he had long ago despaired of being able to convince Milly Duffrin of that. He had virtually no interest in the colonial past of the Brewsters or of anybody else; he had no interest in anything that happened in Berryville after the last of the Indian tribes had been dispersed. Since childhood, when he started digging up arrowheads in the woods around Berryville, Brewster had been fascinated by what Berryville must have been like before it had been seen by the Brewsters or the Duffrins or any other white people — unless, of course, it had once been seen by white explorers from Scandinavia, whose implements Brewster always dreamed about discovering, or by some Stone Age forager running from a dinosaur, whose bones Brewster fantasized about finding in a tidal pond and assembling with the aid of only an anatomy chart and a few volunteers from the high school. The Berryville Museum did have Revolutionary War uniforms and colonial weather vanes, but a visitor had to work his way through a lot of arrowheads to find them.

"I know why this museum was set up, Sam Brewster," Milly Duffrin went on. "So that little mayor could make everyone think that the history of Berryville went right from the savages to a bunch of foreign factory workers."

Brewster only shook his head, being unwilling to find out how Milly Duffrin might react to hearing the real cause of the museum's founding — which concerned neither archeology nor colonial history but an attempt by Mayor DiCarlo to obtain some federal funds for improvements to the municipal water-treatment plant. The mayor had been informed by a consultant in federal programs that some federal money earmarked for cultural development in towns of a certain size could be obtained easily and could, with some mild manipulation of the fine print, be diverted to water-treatment plant renovation. Only the first half of the advice turned out to be correct. The mayor, finding himself with a grant that could only be used to establish a museum, either had to establish a museum or return the money. Sam Brewster had been delighted to take an early retirement from the family hardware business and become the museum's curator. The hardware business had never held much interest for him beyond the opportunity it presented to leaf through catalogues that occasionally offered sophisticated digging tools. Even before his retirement, he thought of himself less as the co-proprietor of a hardware firm than as the Founder and President of the Berryville Archeological Society.

"You're too stubborn to argue with, Samuel," Milly Duffrin said, and she marched up the stairs, just as Duane Minnick and Clifford Bates came down and approached Brewster's desk.

"If any new dirty books have arrived, they'd be upstairs in the library," Brewster told them. "This is the museum down here."

"We got something for you to look at, Mr. Brewster," Clifford said.

"Yeah, we think it's some kind of thing like all that Indian shit you're always digging up," Duane said. Clifford poked Duane painfully in the biceps with the rock as a signal to keep his mouth shut.

"Well, let me have a look at it," Brewster said. He knew that his inclination to be short with Duane and Clifford might be based on impatience he had stored up while waiting in his car at Earl's Texaco, drumming his fingers on the steering wheel, while Duane tried to copy numbers on a credit-card receipt and sing a country song at the same time. Brewster actually had nothing against the two boys. In fact, if the town gossip about who had switched the No Trespassing signs on Gerald Baker Manley's property was correct, he admired their daring and agreed completely with their sentiments. Having always believed that a number of clearings on the Manley property were logical places to search for Indian eating utensils of the sixteenth century, he was infuriated when the electrified fence had, as he put it at an Archeological Society meeting, "closed the area to scholarly research."

Clifford Bates deposited the stone on Brewster's desk. Brewster picked it up and studied it. Then he put it down, got out a large magnifying glass, and began studying it again. Then he put the stone and the magnifying glass down, got a soft cloth out of his desk, rubbed the stone carefully, picked up the magnifying glass, and began studying it again. Duane and Clifford tried to restrain themselves from leaning over Brewster's shoulder to see what he was looking at.

"Some sort of real valuable Indian shit, I guess," Duane finally said.

"Shhh," Clifford said, and gave Duane an elbow in the upper arm.

Even without the magnifying glass, Brewster was able to see the inscriptions on the stone clearly — two lines of symbols, the symbols divided up into what were obviously words. Trying to control his excitement, he put the stone down on the desk, went up to the library, and returned a few minutes later with a large book. He compared the symbols on the stone to the symbols in the book. Then he closed the book and — speaking extremely slowly, the way people sometimes speak in an emergency to guard against panic — he asked Duane and Clifford precisely where they had found the stone, taking notes on their answers. Then he picked up his magnifying glass and stared at the stone again. "Unquestionably runic," he murmured, half to himself. "Runic beyond a shadow of a doubt."

"I never heard of Runic Indians," Duane said.

"If there weren't many of them to hear about, their stuff must be worth a fortune," Clifford said. "Supply and demand."

"Not Runic Indians," Brewster said. "Runic writing. The writing on this stone is undoubtedly in the runic alphabet."

"And the people who wrote runic weren't called Runics?" Clifford said.

"They weren't called Runics and they didn't write runic," Brewster said, and, with only occasional glances at the book in front of him, he explained to Duane and Clifford at some length how the runes were an alphabet that came to be used by the common people of northern Europe in the Middle Ages to write such languages as Old Norse — often on stones.

"Well, we don't have anybody around here who'd be an Old Norse," Duane said. "We got Italians. We got Armenians. Mr. Derounian at the Yankee Cafe is a full-blooded Armenian. We got French-Canadians."

"We're up to our asses in French-Canadians," Clifford said.

"The people I'm talking about aren't here now," Brewster said. "The vital point is this: Were they here in the Middle Ages?"

"I don't know what they'd be doing here with a bunch of Indians," Clifford said.

"Burying arrowheads and shit like that maybe," Duane said.

"Viking explorers are known to have left runic inscriptions on stones," Brewster explained. "And Viking explorers certainly reached the shores of North America. But never has a fully authenticated runestone been found to prove once and for all where Leif Ericson and his men really landed."

"So this rock could mean there were explorers here?" Clifford asked.

"It could mean much more than that," Sam Brewster said. "It could mean that Berryville is Vinland."

Duane and Clifford had, as they told Brewster, been alone when they found the stone with the weird writing on it — alone but, as it turned out, not unobserved. Gerald Baker Manley was on the porch of his summer house, peering through his telescope. His wife, Blake Pierson Manley, had once taken it for granted that he used his telescope for bird-watching, as a way to relax from the strain of litigation. She had enjoyed teasing him mildly about how the grackles were getting on. As it turned out — she had learned after the desecration of the No Trespassing signs — Manley spent his hours on the porch with his telescope watching for trespassers, like a World War II merchant marine commander scanning the ocean for signs of U-boats.

Manley hated trespassers. He had been so upset over the incident involving the No Trespassing signs that his wife was concerned that, for the first time, he might allow his concentration in court to be affected. At the time, Manley was defending a trio of teenagers accused of defacing the Boston subway with spray-painted graffiti. His defense had, in fact, been brilliant. He had called to the stand an awesomely articulate Boston University professor of communications arts who testified that, viewed outside "the culture-lock of middle-class values," the graffiti could be considered poetry — one of its poems ("LeRoy is de King") being "a classic of its type." Manley had argued eloquently that graffiti was a First-Amendment-protected right. He had also found a precedent for wall-writing in a Massachusetts Bay Colony law, still on the books, giving each male resident the right to "Inscribe in such manner as he shall see fit publick boards and barn dwellings." The teenagers were acquitted. Manley enjoyed the triumph and the press interviews, but he could hardly wait to return to Berryville and his telescope.

He was playing the telescope over the dwarf pines and patches of beach grass near the electrified fence. He loved his property. As a child he had lived in a cramped apartment in Boston. Manley was the grandson of a Czech immigrant whose surname had been bestowed upon him by a sympathetic immigration officer who knew what an added burden a name with no vowels at all might be in America. Manley's own father, a druggist with occasional flashes of irony, gave his son the middle name of Baker as a gesture to the original Manley, who had made his living in America baking Czech pastries. During Gerald Baker Manley's childhood, his family had no interest in owning a country place, since it was understood that the drugstore could not be left for so much as a weekend in the complete control of the mildly untrustworthy cousin who shared its management. Manley's first taste of country life had come with his marriage to Blake Pierson, a member of a wealthy Boston family renowned for its prominence in banking and government. The Piersons had been established so long, someone once reported to the regulars gathered for coffee at the Yankee Cafe, that they even had a Latin motto; Art Norton had said that it translated into "The Rewards of Public Service Are Cushy Ambassadorships."

"I think there's something out there!" Manley shouted. "Out by that point. Movement!"

Blake Manley came out on the porch and looked

through the telescope. "Grackles, Gerry," she said. "Those are grackles, and I wish you'd spend a relaxed few moments looking at them." Blake Manley liked privacy herself, but she had found her husband's near-obsession with land-protection puzzling. He had been absolutely unwilling to discuss her contention that installing an electrified fence was a showy and needlessly expensive way of doing a job that could be done every bit as well by barbed wire.

What Blake Pierson Manley did not know was that her husband was possessed by a Grand Plan for a summer community. The Grand Plan had been born only half a dozen years before, when Manley discovered Berryville. According to the sign at the city limits, Berryville, Heart of the Yankee Shore, had been discovered in 1702 — but not the way Gerald Baker Manley discovered it. Despite the lovely coves of its huge harbor, despite its proximity to Boston, Berryville had never attracted summer people. It had always been known as an industrial town, almost solely because of a huge tractor-gear plant that, from the time of its construction in 1894 at the point of a strategic peninsula, had dominated the harbor — looming into view whenever anyone looked up from even the most remote and picturesque cove. The plant had fallen into disuse in the twenties, and had remained an empty, horrifyingly ugly red-brick hulk for years thereafter, despite the efforts of a series of Industrial Development

Commissions to find a use for it. The tractor-gear plant had been the first building Gerald Baker Manley saw when he happened to pass through Berryville while out on a drive to relax from the pressures of a civil liberties case he was arguing in a nearby town — the case of an elementary school teacher of progressive views who claimed that she was fired by the local school board solely because she had refused to teach her students to spell.

Manley had recognized the tractor-gear factory as an obstacle that could be dealt with one way or another once the land in the coves it overlooked had been bought. He knew from his wife that windows and cornices and even bricks from nineteenth-century buildings were gradually becoming valuable. If worse came to worse, he figured, he could buy the building, tear it down, sell its component parts, and more than make up the loss with the appreciation of land it had overlooked. As it happened, that proved to be unnecessary. Mayor DiCarlo, having been led to believe that grants from the Economic Development Administration were often flexible enough to be used for such projects as the modernization of a water-treatment plant near the site of economic development, had applied for a grant to transform the tractor-gear plant into the Yankee Craft Centre and Shopping Mall. To his astonishment, a check for the full amount applied for had arrived almost immediately —

23

accompanied by a particularly inflexible contract and an on-site compliance officer. Three years after Manley bought his fourteen acres near Sandy Thumb, the renovation had given the exterior of the factory precisely the appearance it had when it began keeping summer people away in 1894, and Blake Pierson Manley was able to say that her summer house had "an absolutely marvelous view of a perfectly restored nineteenth-century tractor-gear factory."

Manley's Grand Plan went further than merely buying fourteen acres before their value had benefited from a change in the view. He had envisioned friends and acquaintances buying up other coves to establish a small, compatible summer community — small because, given the number of acres Manley considered necessary for a respectable parcel of land, there would be room for only fifteen families or so. All of the coves would be protected. There would be no room for the tacky beach cottages or crowded beaches that his wife despised. The people who lived in the community would build the rambling weathered-shingle houses that Manley had admired since he first visited the Pierson compound near Bar Harbor. They would gather occasionally, informally of course, at one house or another to have drinks. They would discuss world problems and the constitution and private schools. At the center of the group would be the founder of the community — not some stuffy Pierson who insisted on being called Mr. Ambassador but the well-known civil liberties lawyer, Gerald Baker Manley.

The Grand Plan, in fact, was gradually working out. Furiously taking options and searching titles, Manley had been able to preside over the purchase of just about all of the appropriate land — the exception being Sandy Thumb, whose ownership seemed buried in baffling layers of contested wills and family feuds and disputed titles. Most of Manley's neighbors were precisely the right sort of people. The community included a foundation executive and two law professors and a wellborn left-wing writer and even a Jewish intellectual — an ancient and somewhat deaf but still renowned poet and philosopher named Schmule Rifkind. His neighbors, Manley thought as he peered once again through his telescope, were the sort of people who could discuss graffiti but would never scrawl any. They were intelligent people who could grasp an issue. Once he managed to get an option on Sandy Thumb, he would approach them on the possibility of extending the electrified fence to the perimeter of the community's holdings.

"Sandy Thumb!" he shouted suddenly. "Trespassers nearing Sandy Thumb. Get the police chief on the phone, Blake. Trespassers!"

"Gerry, please," Blake Manley said, as she rushed out on the porch. "They're not on our land. We don't even own Sandy Thumb."

"They're just waiting until my back is turned," Manley

25

said, keeping his eye to the telescope. "Jesus! I think those must be the two little delinquents who vandalized my signs. Trespassing bastards!"

"Gerry, it can't be trespassing if they haven't come onto our land."

"Conspiracy to trespass," Manley said. "That's what's going on right now out there — conspiracy to trespass."

"You told me all conspiracy laws were repressive," his wife said.

"Every society has the right to protect itself against terrorism," Manley said. "Just wait till I get my fence out there!"

"Don't worry about getting that pothole on Main Street fixed, Your Honor," Art Norton said, as he entered the Yankee Cafe at eight-thirty on the morning after Duane and Clifford made their discovery. Norton sat down next to Mayor DiCarlo at the table reserved for the businessmen's morning coffee gathering. "I'm sure they'll get that poor guy out of there somehow," Norton went on. "I just hope they don't have to call in scuba divers to find him. He's down in there pretty deep."

Art Norton was, by unanimous agreement, the most accomplished ribber among the regulars who were found drinking coffee in the Yankee Cafe every weekday morning. Norton's comments about goings on in Berryville were carried home at the end of the day by Yankee Cafe regulars like bouquets — which is about the only way anyone outside the Yankee Cafe heard them, since Norton's editorials in the *Advance* never included what the paper's owner called "downbeat stuff." The *Advance* was owned by Berryville's most tireless booster, John R. Sprigg III, who was also a board member and part owner of the Berryville Trust Company, chairman of the Economic Development Commission, and chairman of the Executive Committee of the Chamber of Commerce. Sprigg — who was known around town as Johnny-Three, to distinguish him from his late father, who had held precisely the same positions — believed the duty of a newspaper was to stress the positive aspects of its hometown. It was often said in Berryville that for finding out what was going on around town five minutes of listening to the gossip at the Yankee Cafe was worth five years of subscribing to the Berryville *Advance*. "We are a newspaper that prizes discretion above all other virtues," Art Norton sometimes said. "If the mayor and the president of the Chamber of Commerce started screwing goats on Main Street at high noon on the Fourth of July, they would have to keep screwing goats until the national press heard about it if they expected to get their picture in the newspaper."

"I told you we'd have a crew out at that goddamned pothole as soon as we could," Mayor DiCarlo said, as Mike Derounian came over with three cups of coffee and sat down. The Yankee Cafe's regular waitress, Heather Palermo, had called in sick, and Derounian was handing out the coffee himself until a fill-in for Heather arrived.

"That guy down in the pothole didn't look like a roof repairman on his way to a job, did he, Art?" Derounian said.

"Just hand out the goddamned coffee, will you, Mike?" the mayor said. "I'm in a hurry."

The rest of the regulars started drifting into the Yankee Cafe — Henry LaDoux from the drygoods store; Vinnie Marchetti, the owner of Amos W. Barnes & Sons, Chemists (Est. 1873); Frank Kelley of Sargent & Wainscott, Real Estate; Roy Bouchard, who ran the camera and hobby shop. A lot of the businessmen in Berryville were from immigrant families that had, for one reason or another, drifted over from nearby mill towns to take over first City Hall and eventually most of the Main Street businesses from the old Yankee families that had been in Berryville since the eighteenth century. The transition had been so gradual that the tone of the town was left practically unchanged — the Italians and Irish and French-Canadians having unconsciously acquired the Yankee customs that went with the hardware stores and real estate offices. Berryville continued to call itself "Heart of the Yankee Shore." When tourists passed through, they found qualities of flinty New England independence in people who were, in fact, likely to be the sons and daughters of French-Canadian mill-workers or Italian bricklayers. An outsider who happened to wander onto the Berryville public dock invariably came away with stories about the taciturnity of an ancient Yankee whittler — a man whose name happened to be Guido Popolizio and whose tendency toward silence happened to be based on his being a Genoese who spoke not a word of English. Mayor DiCarlo himself was the captain of Berryville's Colonial Drum and Bugle Corps, and genuinely hated King George III of England.

"I would have been here sooner," LaDoux said, "but they thought the guy down in that pothole might need some warm clothes, so I dropped a parka down there." DiCarlo just grunted.

"What's this I hear about the Minnick kid finding some rock?" LaDoux went on. "I hear he took something into Sam Brewster yesterday afternoon and Sam thinks it's the Hope diamond or something."

"The Minnick kid in the Army that hit his sergeant?" Marchetti asked.

"No, the one that works at Earl's Texaco," LaDoux said. "The dumb one who's always pretending the gas hose is a guitar."

"The author of 'Your Plugs Have Set a Spark Off in my Heart' and other country classics," Art Norton said.

"That kid couldn't find his way home," Marchetti said.

"Well, Derounian heard that he found some kind of Danish rock or something," LaDoux said.

The arrival of John Houghton, the manager of the

local utility company, stopped the rock conversation. It was customary to greet Houghton with two or three minutes of mock complaints about the electricity service, in the same way the mayor was greeted with pothole jokes and Dr. Frank Trimani, a local general practitioner, always had to listen to four or five remarks on the policy he supposedly followed of prescribing two aspirin for diseases ranging from compound fractures to beriberi — a policy that had earned him the nickname of "Take Two" Trimani. LaDoux had just repeated his theory that the only explanation for an electric bill as high as he had just paid was the light in the freezer remaining on after the door was closed ("I think the company should send a responsible executive over to climb in and check it out, Houghty") when Sam Brewster walked into the Yankee Cafe.

Brewster had spent some time thinking about how the news of the runestone should be broken to the mayor and the merchants of Berryville. He knew he would find a number of them in the Yankee Cafe between eight-thirty and nine, and he knew they would be a difficult audience. He liked a lot of the Yankee Cafe regulars — he had gone to school with some of them, and he had often showed up at the Yankee Cafe for morning coffee himself when he was in the hardware business — but he thought of them as Philistines. They enjoyed joking about people's professions. When Marvin Rappaport, the local dentist, dropped into the Yankee Cafe, he was invariably greeted as "Fat Fingers." Brewster's own arrival often inspired stories about dogs being found chewing on genuine Indian-chief bones. On some mornings, the conversation in the Yankee Cafe seemed to go from jokes about potholes to speculation on the love life of Heather Palermo, Derounian's voluptuous waitress, and back to jokes about potholes. The only serious subject that ever seemed to hold the attention of the Yankee Cafe regulars was Gross Retail Sales.

It occurred to him that the best approach to the subject of runestones might be a rather casual one. The opening that he had, in fact, rehearsed that morning as he shaved had been "One of the Minnick boys stumbled onto something that might be of interest to the town some day, if the proper authentication comes through, which will all take time, of course." He had also considered a more scholarly approach, scholarly but not pedantic, as he saw it: "As some of you may know, scholars have for many years tried to find artifacts that could be considered absolute proof that the Vikings, in their early voyages, reached the shores of what is now the United States. There has been general agreement in the field, of course, that, even in the absence of artifacts, there is little doubt that some of the Northern voyages did reach these shores. However, precisely where the Vikings landed . . ."

At breakfast, he had decided to go back to the casual version, and then had abandoned that for a plan his wife had suggested — joining the group at the Yankee Cafe with no more than a polite good-morning, thereby forcing the regulars to drag the truth out of him. There was no doubt, after all, that they would have some knowledge of the find. The chief librarian, Bertha Winstead, who had seen him scurrying around for sources and must have exacted some information from Duane and Clifford as she bawled them out for dripping water all over her vestibule, was such a gossip that Art Norton always referred to her as the Berryville Information Service. In preparing for the scene at the Yankee Cafe, Brewster had even imagined himself in the role of the scholar being questioned by laymen who tend to oversimplify. "Well, I wouldn't go so far as to say that," he might respond when asked by Larry DiCarlo if Leif Ericson had really camped within the city limits. When Henry LaDoux or Roy Bouchard asked him if the Viking ships had really been right there off Sandy Thumb, he would pull at his pipe once or twice, and maybe pause to light it up again, and then talk a bit about how cartography and the shoreline itself would have been altered enough in eight or nine hundred years to make specific identification of harbors a sort of parlor trick that held no interest for serious scholars.

Having committed himself to the question-and-answer approach, he merely nodded at the regulars as he sat down and started pouring sugar into the cup of coffee Mike Derounian had pushed in front of him.

"Well?" Larry DiCarlo said, in the tone that always implied that the answer would have to be forthcoming immediately if it had any chance of catching him before he was out the door and on his way.

Brewster paused for a second, swallowed, and then almost shouted, "Berryville is Vinland!"

Within two hours of Sam Brewster's appearance at the Yankee Cafe, most residents of Berryville knew that they might be living in Vinland — although many of them were still not quite clear about what Vinland was, or how living in it might vary from living in Berryville. After some thought, Bertha Winstead had chosen Milly Duffrin to be the first person she would telephone with the news, and she was rather disappointed in Milly's lack of enthusiasm. Bertha had forgotten that the only aspect of medieval history that had ever excited Milly had to do with the possibility, suggested in the report of a genealogist she had once hired, that the Duffrins were descended from Charlemagne — a possibility that prompted Mayor DiCarlo to say, "See! Milly Duffrin's a Canuck just like everyone else in this goddamned town." Bertha Winstead tried to make up for her disappointment at Milly Duffrin's bland response by telephoning twelve more people before her morning coffee break.

In the teller's line at the Berryville Trust Company,

Henry LaDoux told Max Hebert, the police chief of Berryville, about the stone that the two boys had picked up near Sandy Thumb, and Hebert told LaDoux that anything Clifford Bates picked up was probably somebody else's property or the clap.

"You've never actually brought him in for anything, have you, Max?" LaDoux asked.

"I never caught him is all," the chief said. "I could have probably proved that Bates and Minnick switched those signs out at Manley's, but since I used to like to go duck hunting out there before that bastard put that fence up, I wasn't exactly working night and day to crack that case."

"I thought they ought to get the Kiwanis Citizen of the Year award for that," LaDoux said.

"Well, also, last year I figured Clifford Bates was probably the one that put that stuff in the City Hall water cooler that made all the secretaries and everybody pee purple," the Chief said. "Also, he may be the one that keeps putting dog shit under the statue of the general out at City Park, so it always looks like the general had an accident."

"You think the stone could be a joke of Clifford's?"

"Maybe," the chief said. "But maybe not. It doesn't seem to have anything to do with bodily functions, and that seems to be Clifford's specialty. Did anyone actually see Minnick bend down and pick up the stone?"

"Not that I know of," LaDoux said. "They were over on the side of Sandy Thumb near where Manley lives, so maybe Manley saw him."

"Probably not," the chief said. "If Manley saw him that close to his property, the crazy son of a bitch would have probably shot his ass off."

Gerald and Blake Manley had not, in fact, been the only witnesses to the discovery of what became known as the Berryville Runestone. In a clearing on a hill overlooking Sandy Thumb, the movements of Duane and Clifford were followed with high-powered binoculars by John Ronald Sprigg IV, the son of Berryville's most prominent businessman. For as long as anyone could remember, the fourth John R. Sprigg had been called Ronnie rather than Johnny-Four — as if it had been apparent, even in infancy, that he would not follow precisely in the footsteps of the Spriggs who preceded him. Unlike the previous John Spriggs, he seemed to have no interest in the bank or the newspaper or the chamber of commerce. His father, John R. Sprigg III, knew virtually everyone in town, and had been seen often enough at Gerald Baker Manley's cocktail parties to be called by Art Norton "the summer people's token townie." Ronnie Sprigg was a loner. Having been away at school for years, he had lost contact with the people in town his own age — many of whom had married and moved just

35

outside of town to Berry Vue Estates. The only towns-person Ronnie Sprigg seemed to spend much time with was a much older man, Alonzo Jones, Berryville's only black resident, with whom Ronnie sometimes passed long afternoons — sitting in a back booth of Jones's restaurant, Wong's Garden of the Orient, and exchanging views on a wide range of subjects while eating Chinese food. Unlike John Sprigg III, an enthusiastic hunter who had dedicated to the Berryville Museum what Art Norton sometimes described as "one of the finest tax-deductible rhino heads on the East Coast," Ronnie Sprigg's interest in the outdoor life was confined to bird-watching. His interest in bird-watching made Ronnie one of the few Berryville residents who might have been expected to be lying in a clearing overlooking Sandy Thumb, peering through binoculars. His interest in bird-watching was also one of the factors that made him, in the minds of many townspeople and the words of Bertha Winstead, "not exactly the average boy next door, if you know what I mean."

Ronnie Sprigg was not actually a boy anymore; he was twenty-eight years old. Everyone in Berryville tended to think of him as a boy partly because he never seemed to finish up his studies and go to work. He was always taking a course in archeology here, a summer session in Chinese Studies there. When asked when he was going to be finished studying, Ronnie always answered politely that he seemed to have a lot to learn. He had always been polite about everything. To most people in Berryville, courtesy seemed to be Ronnie Sprigg's dominant trait. He called Larry DiCarlo "sir" or "Mister Mayor." He always shook hands formally, if silently, with Guido Popolizio. His teachers at Berryville Elementary School, which he attended for a few years before being sent off to boarding school, found him unfailingly polite, and so had every teacher after that. "Very courteous!" John Sprigg III finally exploded one evening, when alone with his wife. "I asked Ronnie's teacher how he was doing and he said Ronnie was 'very courteous.' What kind of thing is that to say about a twenty-three-year-old graduate student in anthropology — 'very courteous'!" It was partly Ronnie Sprigg's courtesy that made some of the Yankee Cafe crowd suspect that he might be what Mayor DiCarlo always called "a little light on his feet."

It was rumored around Berryville that Ronnie Sprigg had the funds to take a course here and there because of a sizable inheritance from his grandfather. The inheritance was the greatest test of John R. Sprigg's promise — reexacted by his wife almost weekly — that he would control his temper while dealing with Ronnie. Since the age of twenty-one, Ronnie had managed the inheritance without a word of discussion with his father. John R. Sprigg, to his constant frustration, did not even know how it was invested. The discretion about financial matters he had acquired as a bank director and the oddly formal relationship he had with his son made it impossible for him to ask outright. Occasionally, he would try to bring up the subject casually at dinner by saying something like, "Johnson, in the trust department down at the bank, is doing very well with some municipals these days."

"How nice for him," Ronnie would say, apparently with absolute sincerity.

"Anytime you want to go through things with any of the fellows down there, of course, don't hesitate to ask," Sprigg would say.

"Thanks very much, father," Ronnie would say. "It's awfully kind of you to offer." John Sprigg would start to grow red in the face, and his wife would kick him under the table to remind him of his promise.

Lying in the clearing above Sandy Thumb, Ronnie Sprigg watched the two boys move slowly toward the boulder near the end of the point. He saw Clifford skip the rock across the water to drench Duane. He saw Duane pick up a rock for retaliation, and then stop to examine it. A goldfinch dived into Sprigg's field of vision. He paused to record it in his journal of sightings. "How nice it always is to see a goldfinch at Sandy Thumb," he mumbled to himself. (Ronnie Sprigg sounded polite even when he was alone.) Then he once again turned his binoculars on Duane and Clifford.

"What kind of story you going to have about this in the *Advance*, Art?" Mike Derounian had asked Art Norton, after Sam Brewster and most of the regulars left the Yankee Cafe.

"Well, you know the *Advance* is an objective newspaper," Norton said. "We are equally inaccurate about both sides."

John R. Sprigg III rarely complained about inaccuracy in his newspaper unless the inaccuracy in question was the misspelling of the name of a close friend or advertiser. There were always a lot of names in the *Advance*, since careful coverage was given board elections of the Chamber of Commerce and the Industrial Development Commission and even some of the boards and committees that John Sprigg did not chair. Name-spelling was Sprigg's principal interest in the editorial side of the *Advance*. When he had taken over the newspaper from his father, at about the same time Gerald Baker Manley discovered Berryville, he promised the staff some modernization. A year or so later, he had seen to it that the newsroom was redecorated in precut sheets of a slick substance that looked more or less like wood. He had also arranged for a college friend who was in industrial design to redesign the *Advance*'s logo — "clean it up a little," as the friend put it — so that it said Berryville *Advance* in simple, modernistic, all-lower-case letters. Except for his constant inspection for downbeat stuff, Sprigg's interest in the news columns of the *Advance* seemed to lie dormant until the discovery of the

Berryville Runestone. He ordered Norton to put the *Advance's* best reporter on the story immediately.

The best reporter on the *Advance* was Jeff Bryant, who had been added to the staff a year before after several years of grumbling by Art Norton that three reporters were not enough as long as one of them "spent eighty percent of her time writing about which board Johnny-Three was elected president of." Bryant had come to the paper right out of journalism school — a cheerful, earnest young man who was once described by Norton as "a bundle of irrelevant enthusiasms." On his first day of work, Bryant had suggested that the *Advance* launch a consumer column — a column that would point out, for instance, price variations in Berryville stores and how the prices in all of those stores compared to the prices offered by discount stores in Portland or Boston. Norton sent him to cover a United Fund luncheon instead. A few weeks later, Bryant wanted to write an exposé of the way the Chamber of Commerce was inflating the population figures of Berryville in its promotional literature.

"Do you happen to know, by chance, who the president of the Chamber of Commerce is this year?" Norton asked.

"John R. Sprigg III," Bryant replied. "Everyone knows that, Mr. Norton."

"And do you happen to know the name of the publisher of this paper?"

"The same John R. Sprigg III."

"In that case," Norton said. "The exposé you propose would be a matter of exposing ourselves. And in this state the usual penalty for exposing yourself in public is to be sent to the state hospital for the criminally insane."

Bryant still liked to talk about "a newspaper's obligation to seek the truth," but a year or so on the *Advance* had calmed him down a bit. Art Norton, not without affection, had presented him with a sign, produced by the composing room, that said, "Seek the Truth and It Shall Make You Poor." Within the limits of the *Advance* Bryant had become a responsible and enterprising reporter — accurate even beyond getting the French-Canadian names spelled correctly when covering Chamber of Commerce luncheons.

Jeff Bryant's story ran under a banner headline that read "Berryville May be Vinland" and a drop-headline that read "Ericson May Have Been Visitor Here":

The discovery of an engraved stone found in shallow water near Sandy Thumb Thursday may indicate that Berryville is the long-sought Vinland mentioned by Leif Ericson and other Viking explorers in the Middle Ages.

The stone was discovered by Duane Minnick, 19, of 52 Corkum Road, while he was clamming with Clifford Bates, also 19, of 13 Parnell Street. Both Minnick and Bates are employed by Earl's Texaco Station on Route One.

Samuel G. Brewster, Curator of the Berryville Museum and

President of the Berryville Archeological Society, has studied the stone, and believes that the inscriptions are written in the "runic alphabet" that was used by Vikings in the Middle Ages. Although claims have been made for other stones found in the United States — including one as far away from the Atlantic Ocean as Heavener, Oklahoma — no American runestone has ever been authenticated by scholars.

Mr. Brewster told the *Advance*, "As some of you may know, scholars have for many years tried to find artifacts that could be considered absolute proof that the Vikings, in their early voyages, reached the shore of what is now the United States."

Mr. Brewster did not discount the possibility that the profusion of local flora may account for the name Vinland, which some scholars translate as Land of the Wine Berries, just as it has been presumed to account for the modern name Berryville.

Mayor Lawrence I. DiCarlo said the city is investigating the possibility of applying for a federal grant to finance a full authentication of the stone. "If Berryville is Vinland, the people of Berryville want to know it," the mayor said.

Duane Minnick, the discoverer of the stone, said yesterday, "I knew right away it was a real weird rock." Minnick, who writes country and western songs, has written a song about the experience entitled "I'd Reach Down in That Icy Water if I Could Only Get A-hold of You."

Art Norton accompanied the article with an editorial — one of a category he explained to Yankee Cafe regulars as "Keep off the grass, unless you absolutely must step on it, in which case the answer lies between one hand and the other hand." It was headlined "Good News for Berryville." It began, "All residents of Berryville have reason to be pleased and proud at the news that our town may be Vinland."

On the morning the runestone story appeared in the *Advance,* Larry DiCarlo was in the Yankee Cafe by twenty minutes to eight, carrying his copy of the paper and a pile of books and government pamphlets on federal grants in the field of American culture and history. "Give me a cup of your best, honey," he said to Heather Palermo, who stood poised before him with waitress-pad and pencil at the ready, as if, after eight or nine thousand coffee orders in a row, he might take it in his mind to ask for an omelet *fines herbes* or an egg cooked precisely three and a half minutes and served on dry whole wheat toast.

"A cup of the best?" Heather asked, blankly.

"He means coffee, Heather," Mike Derounian said, coming over to the table and sitting down next to DiCarlo. "Hiya, mayor."

"Where was she yesterday?" DiCarlo asked, as he watched Heather walk away to get the coffee. What Heather was doing and who she was doing it with when she called in sick was a subject of almost obsessive interest among the Yankee Cafe regulars. It was obvious from looking at her, they had all decided, that she was never sick.

"I don't know," Derounian said.

"Why don't you just come right out and ask her?" Di-Carlo said. "She's too dumb to lie."

"Ask her yourself, Larry," Derounian said.

"If you don't care about keeping track of your own employees, it's no concern of mine."

"I don't suppose you brought any roofing equipment with you this morning, Your Honor," Derounian said.

"I thought I sent Eddie Boudreaux over to fix that roof."

"In the first place, Eddie Boudreaux couldn't fix a cat," Derounian said. "Also, I haven't seen him since he came in here six months ago stinking drunk and proposed to Heather in French."

"Don't worry, we'll get to it," DiCarlo said, starting to take short, hurried sips of coffee between every couple of words. "This other stuff is goddamned important. Do you realize I might be the mayor of the oldest settlement in the United States of America?"

"Or at least the leakiest," Derounian said.

"Do you realize what this could mean?" DiCarlo went on. "Let's just say that it's real."

"You can just stand under it on a rainy day and find out it's real. It's definitely real, Larry."

"Mike, please. I'm talking about the rock. You know I'm talking about the goddamned rock. Forget your little leak for a minute and try to think for the good of the town."

"O.K. Let's say the rock is real," Derounian said.

The mayor spoke softly and slowly, the contrast with his usual delivery giving his words the effect of a shout. "That means Berryville is Vinland," he said, and he leaned back in his chair for a moment, not even in position to bolt for the door.

"You thinking of changing the name?" Derounian asked.

"No, no, we wouldn't have to change the name," Di-Carlo said. "That's not the point. But we would change the motto. I mean, there's no reason for the oldest place in the whole goddamn country to brag about being the heart of the Yankee shore, which happens to be a stupid motto in the first place unless you figure the heart is around the armpit somewhere. We'd have a motto like 'Oldest of Them All' or 'The Cradle of the Nation.' I was talking to Johnny-Three about it last night, and he sort of likes the sound of 'Where the Seed Was Planted.' "

"That sounds like a chapter in one of those sex-education books they wanted to teach down at the school," Derounian said.

"Maybe," DiCarlo said. "Anyway, whatever the motto is, this thing could put the town on the map. Let's face it, Mike, what do we have for industry here now? A couple of outfits crapping around with mobile homes and a pants factory that's about to jump to Texas so they can grab onto some cheap wetback labor. The amount of summer people we have don't amount to squat, and from what the grocers tell me those bastards must send relief teams down to Boston every few days to bring back milk and eggs. Nothing's ever going to come of that tractor-gear factory except those goddamn hippie shops we got in there now making tie-dyed jockstraps or whatever they do. And let's face it, the tourists we get here passing through are mainly some stupid sons of bitches who got lost looking for Kennebunk. But if this place is the Oldest of Them All, the Cradle of the Nation, Where the Seed Was Planted! Jesus!"

A few other regulars — Art Norton, Henry LaDoux, Roy Bouchard, Take Two Trimani — had drifted in and taken seats as DiCarlo finished. "Hey, yeah, Larry's right," LaDoux said. "We could have guided tours to the oldest unfilled pothole in North America. Guided tours with those miners' helmets that have the little flashlight right on them. The kids would go for those miners' helmets."

"People would come in here from all over the country," DiCarlo went on, ignoring LaDoux. "Johnny-Three says the biggest or the oldest or the first is what they're looking for, and he's right. When we were in Florida last year, my wife made me drive twenty miles out of the way to see the Second Largest Totally Mined Phosphate Mine in the Western Hemisphere. Think about that. Phosphate is nothing but bird-shit or something, right? And it's not even there, because it's been mined. So we're driving fifteen, twenty miles to see a place where bird-shit isn't! Not even the biggest place where bird-shit isn't. The second biggest place. So think about how far people would go to see the oldest place in the whole goddamned country. It's historic. It's patriotic. They'll bring their kids to see where the country started. Like Washington, D.C., or Williamsburg or Six Flags over Georgia or one of those. Johnny-Three thinks we could have a festival every year. Festivals draw 'em like flies. Anyway, I gotta run." The mayor had pushed back his chair, and was sitting on the edge of it, quickly sipping the rest of his coffee.

"What if it's a phony?" LaDoux said.

"Sam Brewster told me on the q.t. that it was real," DiCarlo said.

"A few days ago you were saying that Sam Brewster didn't know his ass from a parking meter," LaDoux said.

"I suppose it would only be a coincidence if this one turned out to be from Abercrombie and Fitch too," Art Norton said.

"My kid says they have machines that can date when a rock was scratched," Derounian said. "On the other hand, my kid says a lot of screwy things these days."

"No, he's right," Trimani said. "There are carbon-dating machines that can sometimes show at least whether a rock has been inscribed recently or hundreds of years ago."

"Right," DiCarlo said, standing up and walking toward the door. "I'll see you guys later. I gotta run."

"Of course using one of those machines would require having the rock," Norton said.

The mayor walked two more steps. Then he stopped. He turned to Norton. "What do you mean — 'having the rock'?" he asked.

"I mean having it, as opposed to not having it," Norton said.

DiCarlo came back to the table and sat down on the edge of his chair. "Who doesn't have it?" he said.

"Everybody doesn't have it, Larry," Norton said. "Or, to put it another way, nobody has it."

"What are you saying?" DiCarlo said loudly.

"Please don't pound the table or stamp your foot, Larry," Derounian said. "It might make the leak worse."

"Nobody has it?" the mayor almost shouted.

"Nobody we know of," Norton said. "Our intrepid reporter, Jeff Bryant, went out to talk to Duane Minnick under the assumption that at the very same time our slightly less intrepid but very reliable photographer, Frank Petrelli, was going to the museum to get a photograph of the stone. But Petrelli, not finding the stone at the museum, assumed that Bryant was bringing it into the office from Minnick's to have its picture taken. By this time, we had to go to press without a picture. From what I've been able to gather since, it may be that Brewster thought Minnick had it while Minnick thought Brewster had it. It also may be that your plan to transform Berryville into Vinland has had it."

"The goddamned rock is missing!" DiCarlo shouted.

"That's not precisely the headline we had in mind for tomorrow's story," Norton said. "But it's close."

Sam Brewster thought he might smoke his pipe — something he often did in moments of stress. He filled the bowl, looked around his desk for a match, and, not finding one, stood up and started patting his pockets for the lighter he sometimes carried. At that moment, Larry DiCarlo came down the steps into the museum at a half-run. "I know what you're going to say, goddamn it," DiCarlo shouted. "You're going to say, 'I know I had it here somewhere,' and if you do, so help me, I'm going to fire your ass from this museum forever."

"I was looking for a light," Brewster said.

DiCarlo handed him a book of matches. Then he let his breath out slowly, a device Dr. Trimani had recommended for restraining the temper. Then he sat down in the chair facing Brewster's desk and said, "Start at the beginning, Sam."

"Well, in the eleventh century, the Scandinavians, thinking of expansion, built great ships —"

"Not that beginning, Sam," the mayor said. "The beginning when those two little punks brought that rock in here. What happened then?"

"Well, I examined the stone with a magnifying glass. And then I went upstairs to get a book on runic writings —because I could tell right away, Larry, that a rune-stone was what it was, even though the two of them kept babbling on about Indians. Then I compared some letters in the book to the letters inscribed on the stone. That's about it, Larry."

"But who had the stone when they left?"

"Well, I assumed they did. I was very excited, Larry. I can't tell you how excited I was. You don't have a unique archeological treasure handed to you by a couple of grease monkeys every day in the week, you know. I remember that I had gone back to the book on runic writing, and I had become engrossed in a very interesting section having to do with how to distinguish Early Scandinavian, or Urnordisk, from Common Scandinavian, or Fellesnordisk. And I looked up, and they were gone."

"Think back, Sam," DiCarlo said. "Try to remember what happened. Try to remember what was going through your head."

Brewster sat at his desk and tried to concentrate. He remembered that just after he had said, "It could mean that Berryville is Vinland" his mind had become filled with paragraphs from the report he would give of that very moment in history to the Berryville Archeological

Society and, someday perhaps, even to the American Archeological Association — at an annual convention in New Orleans, he hoped, so he could combine the trip with a flight across the Gulf of Mexico to the ruins of Uxmal and Chichén Itzá. He had turned his attention back to the book and the two boys had left and the stone . . . the stone?

Brewster's pipe had gone out. He again patted all of his pockets in an unsuccessful search for a match or a lighter. DiCarlo handed him another book of matches. "I suppose you're quite certain that Duane doesn't have the stone," Brewster said.

"Johnny-Three's over there talking to him now," DiCarlo said. John Sprigg's office had been DiCarlo's first stop after he ran out of the Yankee Cafe. Sprigg, it turned out, had read the entire runestone story on the front page that morning — disproving the prevailing theory in the newsroom that he never went further than glancing through the *Advance* for mentions of his own name — but had been unaware of what the lack of a photograph implied. Alarmed at the news that the greatest industrial development opportunity of all may have been lost, he had agreed to divide up the search — setting out in his Mercedes toward Earl's Texaco as the mayor started toward the Berryville Free Library in his pickup.

"Larry," Brewster said. "I hope if you do decide to

start pounding the table or anything, you'd do me the favor of avoiding that case near the door. The pots in that one are extremely fragile."

"I'm not going to pound the goddamned table," Di-Carlo said. "Jesus, why did it have to be those two imbeciles who found the thing? Of all the people who have been in that cove for the last seven hundred years, that Minnick kid has got to be among the top ten dumbest. Why couldn't the damned thing have washed up in front of you or Milly Duffrin or somebody?"

"Well, I suspect Milly would have translated it on the spot as saying that the Vikings were served tea by a very nice local family named the Duffrins, and then thrown it back in the ocean to guard against other interpretations," Brewster said. "Duane, at least, may have just misplaced it."

"Young man, I want you to remember very hard," John R. Sprigg III was saying to Duane Minnick. "This may be vital to your own future and the future of your hometown, and it may have immense value to the entire scientific community. Do you understand that?"

"Shit, yes, Mr. Sprigg," Duane said. "I sure do."

The morning business at Earl's Texaco had not been heavy when Sprigg arrived, and Duane Minnick was using the slow time to put a new set of wide-track radials on his own shiny Pontiac. He continued working while he answered Sprigg's questions, humming "I Ain't Bowlin' in Your Bowlin' League No More" whenever there was a pause in the conversation. John Sprigg, a large man somewhere in the transition from bulky to stout, paced up and down the length of the Pontiac while asking his questions. Sprigg had once attended Harvard Business School, and ever since he had put great store in the power of deductive reasoning and systematic thinking. He was confident that he would be able to extract the truth from Duane Minnick by a series of detailed, interlocking questions.

"Then you didn't have the stone with you when you left the library?" he was asking for the third time.

"No sir, I sure didn't."

"Why are you so certain?"

"Well, at the vestibule, Miss Winstead bawled out me and Clifford for getting water on her floor. That was when we came in. So we took off our boots. So then when we went out, I picked up one of my boots in one hand and the other boot in the other hand. Then I had my clam rake in one hand, so that doesn't leave any hand for the rock."

Sprigg stood silently for a minute or so. Duane went on with his tire-changing and his singing, using the tire-iron occasionally when he felt the need of a thwack-thwack. Sprigg started to pace up and down again. Suddenly, he stopped. "But that's three hands," he said.

Duane looked down at his hands. There were two of them. "What's that, Mr. Sprigg?" he asked.

"To have one boot in one hand and the other boot in the other hand and your clam rake in the other hand, you needed three hands. And you only have two hands."

Duane thought about it for a moment. "You know, you're right, Mr. Sprigg. That must be why I can't find my other boot. I was looking for my clamming boots this morning, and I could only find one of them. I must have left the other one in that vestibule."

"We'll see," Sprigg said. He strode to his Mercedes. Then he drove straight to the Berryville Free Library, where, in the Lost & Found, he discovered Duane Minnick's other boot.

"I don't think we've ever had one adult boot turned in before, Mr. Sprigg," the assistant librarian told him. "I was wondering — what did you have on your other foot at the time?"

"It is not my boot," Sprigg said stiffly. He thought back over his conversation with Duane, trying to find the flaw in his series of questions. What Sprigg, in his concentration on deductive reasoning, did not think of considering was where Duane Minnick had suddenly come up with the money to buy an entire set of new wide-track radials.

When the tires were all on the Pontiac, Duane Minnick got in and drove to the offices of the Berryville

Advance, where he went into Art Norton's office and offered to sell the paper a picture of the Berryville Runestone. Art Norton examined the picture carefully. It was just a Polaroid shot, but it was clear and well-defined. The inscriptions could be read easily with the naked eye. Norton turned the photograph over in his hand.

"Have you had this picture all along, Duane?" he said.

"Only since we found the stone, Mr. Norton," Duane said. "Clifford said if it was some of that Indian shit we thought it was at first, maybe we ought to get a picture of it so we could take the picture around to show the summer people instead of carrying the stone around. We didn't know anything about any of that Viking stuff. There was plenty of sun for a picture right then, and I always keep that Polaroid in the glove compartment of my Pontiac."

"May I ask why you keep a Polaroid in the glove compartment of your Pontiac, Duane?" Norton said. "I don't suppose you keep it handy just in case you happen to spot a rare osprey feeding in the marshes."

Duane looked down at the floor and blushed. "Well, you know," he said.

"Don't tell me. Let me guess," Norton said. "You and Clifford are collaborating on a photographic essay on New England flora."

Duane looked around the newsroom. "Just between us?" he said, lowering his voice.

"Just between us."

"Well," Duane said, keeping his voice low. "I keep a Polaroid in the glove compartment because a certain lady of my acquaintance likes to pose outdoors sometimes for, well, art poses she calls it."

"Well, I think it's thoughtful of you to use a Polaroid when you take porn shots of Myrna McDonald," Norton said. "If you took film like that to Roy Bouchard at the camera shop he'd probably get a double spasm in his prostate region just thinking about what the lab refused to print."

"I didn't know you knew about Myrna," Duane said.

"The notion that we are totally ignorant here about the local scene is only an impression some may get from reading our newspaper," Norton said. "May I ask why you didn't tell Mr. Sprigg about the photograph?"

"He didn't ask me," Duane said. "All he seemed to want to talk about was my clamming boot."

Norton considered what the conversation between Duane Minnick and John Sprigg III at Earl's Texaco must have been like. For the first time, he felt he appreciated what some Washington reporters meant when they said that they would have liked to have been "a fly on the wall" during certain historical confrontations. "And you'd like to sell this photograph to the paper, would you?" he said.

"Yes sir," Duane said. "From what I read in the *Advance*, I guess the rock turned out to be pretty valuable."

"Well, we usually pay Frank Petrelli five dollars for a

shot of the United Fund board of directors or the new trustees of the hospital or some similar historical gathering. Of course, this is what you might call a rare photo."

Duane smiled and nodded.

"On the other hand," Norton went on. "We pay to a certain extent according to the experience and seniority of the photographer. And this would be your first picture in the *Advance* — the first picture we would have published that said 'Photo by Duane Minnick' under it. Unless, of course, you prefer to use a middle initial."

"No, Duane'd be O.K."

"Frank Petrelli does have considerable experience in the field. I would say that Frank Petrelli has taken pictures of perhaps four or five hundred directors of the United Fund by now — some of them the same directors, of course — not to speak of several hundred award-winning graduates of Berryville High School. Lord knows how many chairwomen of teas. An impressive number, I'm sure. On the other hand, I think I would be safe in saying that nothing Frank Petrelli has taken a picture of for the *Advance* has had any archeological significance whatsoever, and I include the chairwomen of the teas in that statement. No archeological significance at all. So, all and all, I think I could say that the *Advance* would be prepared to make an exception in its normal rate for first-time photographers in this case and pay you ten dollars for this picture."

57

Duane looked disappointed. "There's a four-album set of Country Classics on eight-track at Mr. Bouchard's for thirteen ninety-eight," he said.

"Sold," Norton said, and wrote out a check.

After some reflection, Duane decided that the credit line on the runestone picture should read "Photo by Duane Dale Minnick." For a first effort, it was a remarkable success. There were so many requests for prints that John Sprigg III decided the *Advance* could use the situation to some advantage for advertising promotion. For twenty-five cents, the *Advance* began offering an eight-by-ten matte-finished print of the stone under the legend "The Berryville Runestone tells the world that Berryville is 'Where the Seed Was Planted.' The Berryville *Advance* tells a tri-county audience about help wanted, used cars, and houses to rent. For *Advance* want-ads, phone 637–9500."

One of the first people to purchase a print was Gerald Baker Manley. For Manley, the significance of the Berryville Runestone was not in its implication that Berryville might have been discovered by Vikings but in its implication that Berryville could be discovered by curiosity-seekers, beach-litterers, and, worst of all, trespassers. For a day or so after Duane found the stone, the rumors were encouraging; the stone seemed to have been safely misplaced. But its disappearance and reappearance, at least photographically, seemed to have compounded its notoriety. The first item in the *Advance* about the stone's discovery had inspired only a few short wire-service stories, buried in the Around New England sections of the Boston papers. But the news that someone might have thought the stone important enough to steal quickened the interest of the press. The day after the news of the stone's disappearance ran in the *Advance* — along with Duane's picture, as a refutation to any reader's suspicions that the stone may not have existed in the first place — two out of three network television news shows sent film crews to Berryville from Boston. Both crews, by coincidence, opened with shots of Guido Popolizio. "Berryville is the sort of place where silent old Yankee whittlers spend their days carving the ships of their past," the voice of one correspondent said as the camera played on the hands of Guido Popolizio, who was, as it happens, working on a statue of Saint Antony Gianeli of Genoa. "Now it may be that, before the ancestors of this old Yankee ever arrived, a ship in Berryville's past was commanded by Leif Ericson."

It had taken Manley four telephone calls to find out that only one scholar who could be called a qualified runologist existed on the East Coast — a professor of Scandinavian languages at Harvard named Lars Kulleseid. It required one more telephone call to make an appointment with Kulleseid, who, after warning Manley that conclusions about the authenticity of the Berryville Runestone might be difficult to reach without examining the stone itself, said he would welcome a visit from Manley and an opportunity to see a clearer print than had been available in the Boston newspapers.

"I suppose it's a fake," Manley said, as he handed a copy of the photograph to Kulleseid.

"I suppose," Kulleseid said. He was quite a bit younger and much larger than the picture of a runologist Manley had conjured up in his mind. Spectacles had been a dominant detail in that picture, and Kulleseid did not wear spectacles. He had the sort of calm midwestern voice that was often heard on the public address system of commercial airliners when the pilot comes on to tell the passenger which mountain range is just becoming visible under the left wing. He looked as though he might have played football in college.

"Aren't they all fakes?" Manley asked, noticing, to his mild embarrassment, that a bit of his cross-examination tone had crept into the question.

"Well, all runologists believe that all of the ones found in America so far have been fakes," Kulleseid said. "On the other hand, all Christian theologians believe that all but one of the Messiahs so far have been fakes, so I suppose there could always be a first time." He spent some time studying the photograph; then he took a magnifying glass out of his desk and began studying it again.

Manley drummed his fingers on his briefcase. He could barely restrain himself from an automatic "Have you had sufficient time to familiarize yourself with plaintiff's exhibit?" Kulleseid walked over to the bookcase, withdrew three or four books that had foreign titles, and walked back to his desk. He began studying the photograph again, occasionally referring to one or another of the books. Finally, he looked up from the photograph. "Well, they might take away my little expert's badge for saying so," he said. "But I just don't know."

"You don't know!" Manley was astonished. His experience in questioning specialists came mainly from examining expert witnesses in court, and expert witnesses always knew. They usually knew with absolute certainty. They knew, at least, beyond any reasonable doubt. The professor of communications arts who had identified the poem "LeRoy is de King" as a classic of its type had done so with the certainty of an F.B.I. laboratory technician identifying a clear set of fingerprints.

"I'd sure be interested in seeing the stone if it ever turns up," Kulleseid said.

"But can't you tell it's a fake just from the inscription?"

"I can tell that it's like no other runic inscription I've ever seen, but that doesn't necessarily make it a fake. As you may know, the runic alphabet is pretty simple and the inscriptions on authentic runestones in Scandinavia are always perfectly straightforward; carving in stone isn't a method that encourages wordiness or indirection. Even so, all of the fakes have some obvious mistakes in them. Anachronisms, for instance — two or three letters that had not come into the alphabet at the time the rest of the inscription indicates the message was written, or a word that wasn't in use then, things like that. Or misspellings. And most of the messages don't really make much sense."

"And this one does?" Manley asked.

"No. No sense at all that I can see," Kulleseid said. "But in a different way. The fakes read sort of like a garbled telegram from a teletypist who was drunk, and was never much of a speller sober. Their supporters sometimes claim that the messages don't make sense because they're written in some kind of code, but scholars think they don't make much sense because whoever concocted them didn't know enough about the development of runic letters and the usages in Scandinavian languages to make up a message that doesn't have any errors. The obvious fakes always have some legitimate words in them — often words that can be translated to suggest a description of the place they're found, like 'harbor' or 'cove.' "

"But how about this one?" Manley asked.

"This one, as far as I can tell from a quick first glance, is without anachronism in the letters, and the words aren't close to words I know in Old Norse. There is still no evidence at all that the Vikings actually did use codes — I've always thought it was just a straw grabbed by some of the less rational rune-crazies — but if they did use a code, I suspect it would have looked something like this inscription."

"Are you trying to tell me that this inscription is so far from making any sense that it might be authentic?" Manley asked.

"I guess so," Kulleseid said.

"But maybe this was just done by a particularly clever forger."

"Maybe," Kulleseid said. "But he'd have to be quite learned instead of just clever. And he'd have to have a reason for doing it. It's too much trouble for a practical joke. I don't suppose you have many first- and second-generation Americans up there in Berryville, do you?"

"I don't see that when a person's family came to this country has anything to do with this," Manley said, straightening up in his chair a bit.

"Well, the only reason I ask," Kulleseid said, "is that a lot of the fakes turned up at a time when Swedes and Norwegians in places like Minnesota were being looked down on and called squareheads and all that; whoever carved those fakes probably wanted to show that the Scandinavians were the ones who discovered the place, and weren't just here on sufferance. The Kensington Stone, in Minnesota, was dismissed by all scholars as a fake immediately, but years later it had to be exposed as a fake all over again; everybody had come to believe in it just because so many Scandinavians in the upper Midwest insisted for so long that it had to be real. My relatives were all simple, uneducated farm people out there, people who hadn't been here from Norway very long, and they all believed in the Kensington Stone just about the way they'd believe in some article of religious faith."

"Well, the first- and second-generation Americans in Berryville aren't Swedes, and they all seem to think they're Yankees anyway," Manley said. "And besides, there's no reason for a Swede to be worried about his position in this country now."

"Probably not."

"And what's the difference who was here first?" Manley said. "No decent, liberal-minded person cares about such things anymore."

"I suppose not," Kulleseid said.

"I mean, Columbus discovered America, and he was Italian," Manley said. "Does that make the Italians something special?" He chuckled for a moment at the thought of Italians being something special. Then he stood up to go.

"Well, I wouldn't want to be argumentative about it, Mr. Manley," Kulleseid said. "But, just for the record, Columbus did not, in fact, discover America. We did."

Henry LaDoux settled into his usual chair at the Yankee Cafe. Half a dozen regulars were already at the

table, discussing the translation of the Berryville Runestone and the texture of Heather Palermo's upper thigh
— subjects that were both matters of pure speculation
for all of those present.

"Well, I think I know what that description is going to
end up saying," LaDoux said. " 'Sighted land. Flat and
rocky. Huge pothole.' "

DiCarlo, who was sipping coffee rapidly while standing in his usual half-crouch, ignored the remark. "Johnny-
Three is very hot to change the motto right away," he
said. "Also, he thinks we ought to start planning a runestone festival for this summer."

"Shouldn't we at least wait until they figure out what
the rock says?" Roy Bouchard said.

"It might take months for them to figure out what the
goddamn thing says," DiCarlo said. The mayor's application for federal funds on the basis of Berryville's being a
culturally impacted area had resulted in no funds but
had raised the interest of an arm of government the
mayor always referred to as "an agency I'd just as soon
not name." The unnamed agency had volunteered to put
some of its cryptographers to work trying to decipher
the runic inscription.

"You'd better hurry up with the festival, Your Honor,"
Art Norton said. "Judging by some of its past perfor-
mances, that agency you'd just as soon not name might
decide that the inscription translates into 'A Happy Hol-
iday Season to You and Yours.' "

"How can we have a runestone festival without a runestone?" Bouchard asked.

"The point is the runestone was here," DiCarlo said. "The picture proves that. An important agency of the national government is working on translating it. It doesn't have to be here now. Towns have Mark Twain festivals and Mark Twain isn't there."

"Probably misplaced, poor old soul," Norton said.

"Also, Johnny-Three thinks it'll be easier to float the bonds for the theme-park once we've had a festival," Di-Carlo said.

"What bonds?" four people asked, before anyone thought to ask "What theme-park?"

"Well, you can't just go out and round up nickel-and-dime capital if we're going to build something like Viking Village," DiCarlo said. "It could be I'll figure out some government grant, of course. The S.B.A. and the Economic Development Administration don't seem to be very interested, but I'm talking to a guy with the Department of Forestry this afternoon."

"Where would it be, Your Honor?" LaDoux said.

"I don't know. Maybe at Sandy Thumb if we could ever figure out how to get everyone who owns it to quit arguing long enough to sell it. That's in the future, but we have to get started."

"You sure we need a Viking Village, Larry?" Bouchard said.

"Jesus, yes!" DiCarlo said. "Of course we need a Viking Village, for Christ sake. Johnny-Three says this is the biggest opportunity this town has ever had, and he's right. We've got to think big, Roy. If this is Vinland, you're going to have to start thinking like the descendant of Vikings who sailed the goddamned ocean in wooden ships without fear."

"I happen to be a descendant of French-Canadian farmers," Bouchard said. "With plenty of fear. What they feared most was taxes. What I fear most, as it happens, is also taxes. It's in the genes. For many generations, the Bouchards have known that when people like John R. Sprigg III start talking about great opportunities, people like Roy Bouchard start paying taxes."

"I think Larry may be right for once, Roy," Vinnie Marchetti said. "In the long run, a real tourist industry's going to be great for the tax base. I don't like the idea of paying off bonds either, but this is our one great chance. Tourism is the only answer, and we're not ever going to get many people here to look at Guido Popolizio and those fruitcake sandal-makers in the tractor-gear factory."

"Well, I think we can make the factory part of the overall plan once we get it all figured out," DiCarlo said. "I haven't thought it through, but something like the link between the beginning of the country and the beginning of industry."

"You could always have the fruitcake sandal-makers make Viking sandals," Art Norton said. "Or maybe dress like Viking fruitcakes."

"Don't worry, we'll figure out something," DiCarlo said. "There's a lot in this to draw people. We'll have a rune princess or something, and a parade. Think of all the money to be made just in selling rocks, for Christ sake."

"Selling rocks!" Roy Bouchard said.

"Sure, sure. Selling rocks," the mayor said. "Listen, my wife's cousin brought back a coffee mug from Capistrano, in California, where the swallows come back, and it says, 'Just a swallow from Capistrano.' Johnny-Three tells me there's a place in Colorado or someplace that sells souvenir air. You know, just a can that has some pictures of mountains on it and says Genuine Rocky Mountain Air or something. So why shouldn't the place that has the most important rock in the country sell rocks as souvenirs?"

"Maybe even disappearing rocks," Norton said. "Packaged like Rocky Mountain Air."

"I'm serious," DiCarlo said. "They'll say something like 'Official Authentic Reproduction of the Berryville Runestone' or even just 'I'm a Stone from Berryville.' Something. Christ, Roy, you'll probably be the one that sells the most of them, at the hobby store."

"Well, I guess the Bouchards moved about as many

rocks as anybody in their time," Roy Bouchard said. "But I'm sure this would be the first time we'd ever be involved in selling any."

Gerry and Blake Manley had asked the entire summer colony to their place on Saturday night. Ordinarily, John R. Sprigg III and his wife might have been included on such an occasion, but the Manleys, without saying so to each other explicitly, believed that the evening might take a turn that would make the Spriggs uncomfortable. Since his conversation with Lars Kulleseid at Harvard, Gerald Baker Manley had become increasingly concerned that promotion of the Berryville Runestone could bring hordes of raucous curiosity-seekers to Berryville — he was spending an increasing amount of his time at his telescope, scanning the horizon for their outriders — and he wanted to be able to share that concern frankly with the summer colony.

Porter Fox, the left-wing writer, arrived first, accompanied by his latest girl-friend — Consuela López de la Riviera, an aristocratic Peruvian Communist he had met while researching an article he was writing on the need for land reform in Ecuador. Fox, it was often said in the summer colony, never showed up anywhere without a girl and a petition. The other summer people had come to take it for granted that before any party really got started everyone would have to sign a statement protesting the imprisonment of some poet or the strip-mining of some mountain, and they did it more or less automatically, like big-league baseball players taking a couple of minutes to autograph team baseballs before getting dressed for the game.

Schmule Rifkind, the elderly Jewish intellectual, also arrived early — with his wife, Leah, standing close to him, as usual, so that she could shout in his ear whenever he failed to catch what was said. Rifkind refused to wear a hearing aid on the philosophical ground that what a poet/philosopher needs to hear can not be amplified.

"You're looking absolutely marvelous, Schmule," Manley said, as he greeted the Rifkinds at the door. "Blake and I were just saying that you never seem to age. I suppose it's the mental exercise of keeping on with that writing — the poetry, your history of thought. We think it's great — an inspiration for us all."

"What?" Rifkind said, half-turning to Leah.

"You look good, etcetera," Leah said loudly. Leah was known for her tendency toward compression. It was said that she could have written her husband's seven-volume *History and Inquiry into Thought* in a page and a half.

"There's an interesting commentary on that," Rifkind said, taking off his glasses and concentrating on the problems of polishing them with his coat sleeve while he talked. "I think it was the rabbi of Munchnik, although it sounds much too sensible for him. As you know, I think some of those great eastern European rabbis were the equivalent of mad preachers in the low-church denominations of nineteenth-century Protestanism. Obsessive-compulsives, all of them, and vice versa. At any rate, one of them said, 'An old man has written on his face what a young man can not even write yet on paper.' Now that I think of it, that sounds more like something said by an elder of one of the Plains Indian tribes — when you start to get into it a little deeper, the Sioux and the Hasidim are remarkably difficult to tell apart."

Manley had already turned to greet the next guests. In the few minutes that followed, he had escorted fifteen or twenty people into the room. A warm spring weekend having drawn most of the colony regulars from the city, there were only a few people who did not show up at the Manleys. Cush Montgomery, the foundation executive, was in San Francisco attending a conference on replication. Dominick Searle and Earl Sawyer — a poet and an architect who had been lovers for twenty years in a relationship that was often spoken of among the summer people as much more stable and boring than the most conventional heterosexual marriage — had come to the acrimonious parting of the ways and for weeks had not appeared in public together or separately.

Manley waited until everyone had the opportunity to sign Porter Fox's petition — it denounced inhumane wolf-trapping methods in the Upper Peninsula of Michigan — and to have a drink or two. There had already been some informal conversation about the runestone, of course, but it had melted away after being turned into a monologue by Porter Fox on the foreign policy of the Vikings in terms of twelfth-century geopolitics. "They were expansionist and imperialistic," Fox insisted. "Here they are portrayed in this country in heroic terms and their politics stink. Just stink." The people talking to Fox nodded silently, and then turned the conversation back to the subject of Dominick Searle and Earl Sawyer — the questions under discussion being whether they weren't both better off apart and whether they would ever get back together and who might buy their summer house if they didn't and whether it was really true that the bitterest argument of the separation had to do with which Judy Garland albums belonged to whom.

Finally, Manley stood in front of the fireplace and, raising his voice in a way that made it apparent he was more or less calling the meeting to order, said, "I think we ought to consider what effect this alleged runestone could have on the town." The wife of one of the law professors finished a remark she was making about the possibility that the foundation of the Searle-Sawyer house was settling at a dangerous rate, and then the group grew silent. "I think we have to face the fact that some of the people who run things in the town — the businessmen, that little mayor — are perhaps not the most enlightened people around," Manley went on. "All they're going to be able to see is the short-term profit they might make off exploiting the stone, forgetting the lasting damage they might do to the town in the long run."

"You're absolutely right, Gerry," Porter Fox said. "Essentially the petit bourgeois businessman is no different from the great land exploiters we see in places like Central America. I found in Ecuador, for instance, when you travel deep into the interior, the small merchant at a crossroads store who has been complaining about the land barons will ask an unconscionable price for a pack of Chesterfields. I would never have paid this one bastard, except, as it happened, it was one of those red-hot days you get down there, you know, and —"

"Yes, we do know, Porter," Manley cut in. "I'm sure there are some interesting parallels we can go into sometime."

"What? What?" Schmule Rifkind was saying to Leah in a loud whisper. "What's he saying?"

"Storekeepers are goniffs, too," Leah said.

"What we're talking about here is a lot of shopkeepers ruining a perfectly nice place," Manley said.

"What difference will it all make?" Andrea Fenton, the wife of one of the law professors, said. "We hardly ever go into town except for the paper. The stores are just

73

hopeless. I told one of those grocers I couldn't find any coffee filters and he looked at me as if I had asked him where he keeps the whale blubber. They're just hopeless."

"But, you see, what they're planning is some vast promotional effort, with festivals and souvenir runestones and God knows what else," Manley said.

"What? What?" Rifkind whispered to Leah.

"So let them sell a few souvenir runestones," Andrea Fenton said. "They're probably preferable to the cut of meat you can get in those stores now. Maybe if a few more tourists come into town, the storekeepers will be inspired to allow a piece of fresh fruit within the city limits now and then."

"What?" Rifkind repeated.

"The goniffs don't carry fruit," Leah said into his ear.

"I agree with Gerry," Richard Fenton, Andrea's husband, said. He had a habit of agreeing with anybody who happened to be disagreeing with his wife, but he seemed nearly as concerned as Gerald Baker Manley about the effect the runestone could have. "This could open a whole can of worms," he said. "Pretty soon they'd start talking about building motels. Then the next step is wouldn't it be nice to have some sort of shore road for the tourists, even if you have to come across the property of one or two summer people. Then pretty soon what are the tourists going to do about a decent beach, because once you get into the tourist racket the whole point is to give them more than one attraction so they'll have to stay overnight. I think it's a dangerous business."

"What? What?" Rifkind whispered.

"The stone could be dangerous," Leah said.

"Why dangerous?" Rifkind whispered. But Leah was trying to hear the developing discussion.

"What Dick says is quite true," Manley went on. "I'm particularly concerned about the possibility of demands for public beach access — which I think would be harmful to the beaches and the town in the long run."

"Why dangerous?" Rifkind whispered to Leah.

"Shhh," Leah said, trying to concentrate on what was being said.

"Droves of people would be coming in from all over," Fenton said.

"Droves, no doubt about it," Manley said. "You'd get all kinds of people coming out from the city — and people who were attracted by chintzy promotion and the promise of a cheap outing."

"Why dangerous?" Rifkind said again to Leah.

"Not really the sort of people they think they're going to attract," Manley continued. "And, frankly, not the sort of people you'd want swarming on your beaches, throwing beer cans all over and parading around without any thought of where the public beach ended and the private beach began."

"Why dangerous?" Rifkind almost shouted at Leah.

Leah felt ready to answer. By chance, she picked a moment when there was a lull in the discussion, and, out of impatience with being hectored about it for so long, she herself spoke in what amounted to a shout — leaning over to her husband's ear and screaming, into the silent room, "BECAUSE THE ROCK COULD BRING THE SHVARTZAS."

Jeffrey Bryant of the Berryville *Advance* had arrived at Lars Kulleseid's office only a day after Gerald Baker Manley — working on his own time and at his own expense, of course, since the *Advance* had sent a reporter on an out-of-county trip only once, on the occasion of John R. Sprigg's installation as vice-president of the state Chamber of Commerce. Kulleseid began by recommending two or three books on the Kensington Stone and even one on the Heavener Stone, in Heavener, Oklahoma.

"I recommend that one mainly for its theories on how the Vikings might have sailed their boats from the East Coast to Oklahoma," Kulleseid said. "You'd think that even with the wind right it might be kind of hard to get a boat across the plains of Kansas, but they have it all figured out."

"Someone mentioned a man named Gustafson who's written some books on the subject," Bryant said.

"George Gustafson," Kulleseid said. "He's a very rich

beer distributor from Minnesota. Swedish. He thinks all of the stones are absolutely authentic. Not just the one in Oklahoma, but, as I remember, a couple that have been turned up in Montana. How Leif Ericson managed to sail to Montana is not the kind of thing that would bother Gustafson; the way he talks about how advanced the Viking civilization was, he probably thinks they had helicopters."

"He's not considered very objective by scholars, then?" Bryant asked.

"Well, I went to hear him speak once, out of curiosity," Kulleseid said. "During the question period, someone asked about the possibility that Columbus was here first, and Gustafson said it wasn't worth discussing the possibility that this country was discovered by 'some Italian punk.' I think you'd have to say he's not very objective."

Bryant felt that his own objectivity was still intact. He had admitted to himself from the start that he welcomed the possibility that Berryville — a town that had seemed incapable of producing a national news story or developing a juicy scandal or even becoming funky in an interesting way — might be Vinland. But he believed that the facts had to be investigated thoroughly before a claim could be made, and he had said as much in a critical memorandum he sent to John R. Sprigg III after Sprigg had ordered the motto "Where the Seed Was Planted" run under the *Advance*'s logo. Bryant had also admitted to himself from the start that he was overjoyed at the chance to make a thorough investigation of the runestone. In journalism school, he had majored in Investigative Reporting. The runestone was providing an opportunity to do the type of reporting he had thought he might not have a chance to do until he was, say, the statehouse reporter for one of the Portland (or maybe even Boston) papers — stringing on the side for a newsmagazine or a television network, as he envisioned it, but mainly plugging away in the dusty filing cabinets of the capitol for revealing travel vouchers or shocking bills of sale or highway contracts reeking of nepotism. Neither Art Norton nor John R. Sprigg III had explicitly assigned Bryant the task of getting at the truth of the Berryville Runestone, but he had assumed the task, and assumed the responsibility of making regular reports to Norton on his progress.

"I think I've been looking at all of this in a way that's too complicated," he told Norton one day.

"We try to keep everything in simple sentences here, for the benefit of our slower readers and, of course, the publisher," Norton said.

"I don't mean in the writing of it, Mr. Norton," Bryant said. "I mean I've looked at it this way: The stone may have appeared because the Vikings left it there. If so, O.K. Fine. Berryville is Vinland."

"That seems simple enough," Norton said. "Even for the publisher."

"But then, why did it disappear?" Bryant went on. "Because someone didn't want Berryville to be Vinland. And what if the Vikings didn't leave it there? Then it appeared because someone wanted Berryville to be Vinland — maybe some businessman who had something to gain by all the commercial implications, for instance. And I've been figuring that this person who wanted Berryville to be Vinland made the stone appear and then this other person who didn't want Berryville to be Vinland — someone who thought the peace and quiet of the town would be destroyed, for instance — made it disappear, not realizing that a picture had been taken of it. But why can't they be the same person? Why couldn't whoever made the stone appear also make it disappear — knowing that a photograph would show that the stone had been here but not in a way that could be closely examined, or maybe even knowing that having it disappear would make it even more famous?"

"Complicated, but simple," Norton said. "I suppose you have a list of likely suspects."

"Well, I did make out a sort of list — just people who have something to gain."

"I don't suppose you'd consider it an intrusion, would you, if I asked who was on the list?" Norton said. "I mean, being your editor and all."

"No intrusion at all, Mr. Norton," Bryant said. "You've probably guessed the first name anyway: John R. Sprigg III."

Norton sighed. "Well," he said. "I suppose once you start wanting to expose yourself, it must be the sort of urge that's hard to stop."

"The abalone with fried seaweed is delicious this afternoon, Mr. Jones," Ronnie Sprigg said. "A true marvel. I just don't know how you do it." Sprigg was not merely being polite — although, as usual, polite was one of the things he was being. The Chinese dish he was devouring did strike him as a marvel, and he had no idea how Alonzo Jones, the black proprietor of a Chinese restaurant in a small New England town, managed to produce such masterpieces. Sprigg knew that at the time Jones bought Wong's Garden of the Orient from the Wong family nothing more exotic than chow mein had ever emerged from its kitchen. Sprigg was pretty certain, in fact, that even at their own dinner table the Wongs would have been hard put to go much beyond egg fu yung, since they represented the fourth or fifth generation of the family born and raised in Berryville — the original Wong, according to town legend, having been won in a poker game in Macao by a ship's captain ancestor of Millicent Duffrin. The last of the Wongs in Berryville, Maynard Wong, had seemed to continue the restaurant business mainly because it was expected of him ("If the only Chinese family in town doesn't run the only Chinese restaurant, who will?" he often said), and had jumped at the opportunity to sell out to Alonzo Jones and move to Phoenix, claiming asthma to save face.

Just about everyone in Berryville had assumed that Wong's Garden of the Orient would change greatly under the management of Alonzo Jones, a former short-order cook who, as he grew older, had become what John R. Sprigg III once described to an out-of-town visitor as "philosophical, but not in a dangerous way." But Jones had continued to run the restaurant routinely — so routinely and for so many years, it sometimes occurred to Ronnie Sprigg, that some of the young people in Berryville who hadn't traveled much out of the county might have thought that Alonzo Jones was what Chinese people looked like. According to the menu, Wong's Garden of the Orient served only what it had always served — won-ton soup, chop suey, four varieties of chow mein, and some "American specialties" — but somehow Alonzo Jones could always manage to present Ronnie Sprigg with an exotic and authentic Chinese dish.

"A secret of the Orient," Jones said, smiling. "In point of fact, Mr. Sprigg, a self-educated man such as myself simply learns to extend his research until the true source is reached. Cooking, like any other skill, is within the

reach of applied intelligence; as long as recipes are written down and languages translated, it can not be limited
racially. Maynard Wong, as we both know, was inspired
neither genetically nor environmentally in the kitchen.
He was raised, I've heard, on bologna sandwiches and
Pepsi-Cola. His recipe for won-ton soup, as far as I have
been able to determine, came straight from a cookbook
called *Recipes from and for the American Melting Pot* —
a book teaching the sort of cooking that might be found
in a training school for Methodist missionaries. Naturally, I keep Wong's Special Cantonese Won-Ton Soup
on the menu — most of my customers, poor souls, de-
voutly believe that is what won-ton soup tastes like —
but for special orders such as abalone with fried seaweed I simply consult a better book."

"It's a triumph, Mr. Jones, believe me. A genuine
triumph."

"I'm pleased that you like it, Mr. Sprigg. Without
meaning to boast, I can say that I tend to be pleased
with the special dishes myself — merely as examples of
what can be accomplished by systematic research in a
supposedly esoteric and specialized field. I have a
cousin, you know, who — also with no formal training,
and, needless to say, no applicable ethnic experience —
became a chef in one of those Rumanian-Jewish res-
taurants that used to abound in New York. The kind of
place that uses a lot of garlic and has liquid chicken

fat — schmaltz, in the vernacular — right on the table, for the benefit of customers who feel the need to improve on the chef's excesses, as it were. My cousin learned the job in a week and a half from his predecessor, a Puerto Rican. No problem. I understand that what they used to say about the Jones family in Georgia was 'sassy but smart.'"

"I suppose you've spent a lot of time discussing the runestone in the past few days, Mr. Jones."

"Well, mostly listening, Mr. Sprigg. As you may know, with most of my customers, I just listen. I serve them chow mein and listen. With you, I serve, say, deep-fried sea bass with scallions and I talk. I have done some reading in the field since the stone was found, of course, and I must say that I do find the idea of discovery as a source of ethnic legitimacy rather interesting."

"Discovery as a source of ethnic legitimacy?"

"Yes. In this sense, Mr. Sprigg," Jones said. "Let us take the feeling of Italian-Americans for Christopher Columbus — Columbus Day parades, and that sort of thing. It is all, of course, no different from the feeling the Yankees have about the *Mayflower*, except that the Italians feel a stronger need to prove themselves legitimate than the Yankees do. The Italians obviously suffered at the hands of the people who arrived here in great numbers first and had their own English language established and felt in a position to tell people from Southern

Europe to go back where they came from. It is perfectly understandable that the Italians, anxious for years about proving that they are legitimate Americans rather than foreigners, should insist that America was discovered by an Italian. I can sympathize with their fierce — and, as it turned out, correct — resistance to scholarly acceptance of the Yale map that supposedly proved the Viking familiarity with the shoreline. One can assume that if those 'No Irish Need Apply' signs had prevailed for many more years in Boston the Irish-Americans would have shown more interest than they have in the Irish explorer, St. Brendan, the patron saint of County Kerry, who is thought by some to have reached these shores as early as the fifth century."

"At times, Mr. Jones, I believe that your gift for analysis exceeds even your gift for preparing stuffed bean curd," Sprigg said.

"Thank you, Mr. Sprigg. What I wanted to point out, however, is that the 'discovery' of America is important as a symbolic act rather than as a real accomplishment. For instance, leaving aside the question of how one can be said to have discovered a place in which thousands of Indians have lived for thousands of years, Christopher Columbus discovered America only in the way that Duane Minnick discovered the Berryville Runestone. That is, he stumbled across it while looking for something else."

"An interesting point, Mr. Jones. I don't suppose, by

the way, that you have any of those honeyed apples I so enjoyed for dessert the last time I was here."

"Alas, no," Jones said. "But I do have a little trick with mandarin oranges I've been meaning to show you. I won't be a moment." He went off to the kitchen, leaving Ronnie Sprigg at the table doodling on a Wong's Garden of the Orient paper placemat. Working on the white space between a number of Chinese dragons, Sprigg was idly reproducing the inscription on the Berryville Runestone. The reproduction was remarkably accurate. Sprigg even managed to write with the slightly sloping line that appeared on the stone itself — the kind of line sometimes made by a schoolchild making his first attempts to write on unlined paper.

Alonzo Jones returned to the booth carrying a plate of orange slices that had, by their appearance, been browned in some sort of sugared sauce. As Sprigg began wolfing down the mandarin oranges, Jones studied the runic writing on the placemat. "A very good reproduction, Mr. Sprigg," he said. "But I think you'll find that the last rune in the fourth word — the one that looks a bit like a cross of Lorraine and corresponds roughly to our letter 'o' — should be slightly tilted."

Sprigg studied the fourth word. "I think you're right, Mr. Jones," he said. "That, I believe, is the rune that derived from a rune in an earlier alphabet that looked more or less like a pine tree with one side of its needles missing."

"Correct," said Jones. "I'm sorry; I've forgotten what we were discussing."

"My fault," Sprigg said. "I interrupted when I asked about the apples — for which, I may say, the oranges turned out to be a substitute nearly spectacular enough to blot out thoughts of the original. You were talking about discovery as a source of ethnic legitimacy."

"Oh, yes. What I was about to say is that in a country such as this, where no one but the unfortunate Indians has an absolute claim to legitimacy, there is an understandable temptation to grasp at any source. It makes no real difference, of course, who happened upon this place first — in the dark, as it were, and to no lasting effect — but it's understandable that people think it does. Black people, for instance, have regularly been told to go back where we came from, even though it wasn't our idea to leave where we came from in the first place; once or twice, we've even been offered the passage. So it would be perfectly understandable if, say, black people began to organize national days and all that around the fact that the Pharaoh Necho, who was certainly what would be considered black, sent expeditions to these shores considerably before the Vikings, not to speak of Christopher Columbus."

Ronnie Sprigg looked up from his oranges. "The Pharaoh Necho, Mr. Jones?" he said.

"Yes, the Pharaoh Necho."

"I don't believe I'm familiar with that Pharaoh, Mr.

Jones. That is, I may have heard the name, but I can't seem to place him."

"It might be a fruitful area for your inquiry some time, Mr. Sprigg. Necho ruled around six hundred B.C., and he was a great explorer. Of course, he didn't sail the ships himself, having an entire empire to rule, and all. He often hired Phoenicians and other more or less white people to do the actual seaman's work. There is no doubt in my mind, though, that one of his expeditions landed on the shore of North America."

"Is that right?"

"Yes, oddly enough, that is right," Jones said. "Although to a scholar not driven by ethnic emotionalism, of course, it is a fact of only passing interest."

"Then this inscription," Sprigg said, tapping his finger on the runic writing that appeared on the placemat in front of him. "This inscription could presumably say something like 'Black Men Already Here.' "

"Possibly," Jones said. "Although, of course, that would leave room for the speculation that to the eyes of the light-skinned Scandinavians even the Indians looked black. Also, that would only be four words. The inscription on the Berryville Runestone is clearly six words long. Something like, 'Black seafarers' ships already in harbor.' I believe you'll find that's six exactly."

John R. Sprigg III and Larry DiCarlo, meeting at Sprigg's house as the Chamber of Commerce's Promotion and Development Committee, were having their first serious disagreement involving the Berryville Runestone — whether the young lady crowned at the first runestone festival should be called "Miss Runestone" or "Viking Queen." Sprigg was strongly in favor of "Viking Queen." DiCarlo supported "Miss Runestone" on the simple ground that "Viking Queen" sounded "sort of dike-ish."

"It does not sound dike-ish," Sprigg said. "I don't know where you get that idea, Larry. It sounds fine. You have to realize that 'runestone' is not a very euphonious term. In the first place, 'rune' sounds too much like 'ruin.' Also, who would want to be called Miss any kind of stone? It's a matter of sound and image, Larry. Trust me on this. I'm in the business."

They had been meeting for two hours, and, until the question of what to name the reigning beauty came up, they had been in complete agreement on how to proceed with the festival. It had been agreed that the festival should be held on the first weekend in August — only a few weeks away — to take advantage of the publicity that was generated by the stone's discovery and disappearance. It had been agreed that the Promotion and Development Committee should recommend that the city purchase Sandy Thumb with the intent of developing it into a Viking Village and Beach Recreation Area. It had even been agreed that the Promotion and Development Committee should recommend that the Chamber hire as a consultant Fornus Mitchell, a theme-park designer Sprigg had just heard about — a man who had recently finished a family-entertainment complex in Kansas called Dorothy's Land o'Oz. Everything had been decided except what to call the reigning beauty.

"The Viking image is the right image," Sprigg was arguing. "There's nothing we can do about the fact that the alphabet used for the inscription happens to have an unfortunate name, but we don't have to push it. Viking is what should stick in people's minds. In fact, I'm thinking of changing the motto of the *Advance* to 'Voice of the Viking Coast,' even though I love the sound of 'Where the Seed Was Planted.' "

"I'm sorry!" DiCarlo said, as he paced up and down Sprigg's living room. "Shoot me! What can I tell you? To me, 'Viking Queen' sounds like some great huge bulldike in a fur cape."

Sprigg was silent for a while. Di Carlo continued to pace back and forth. "Now 'Viking Miss' I could go for," DiCarlo finally said.

" 'Viking Princess,' " Sprigg said.

"Done," DiCarlo said. "That's a deal."

The rough wording of the Promotion and Development Committee report having been decided, Sprigg walked DiCarlo to his pickup truck. After the mayor had left, Sprigg stood on his front lawn for a few minutes, taking in the spring evening's air and thinking of how

89

large a supplement the *Advance* might be able to get out as a souvenir program for the Runestone Festival. He was not quite alone. In a lower branch of a large oak tree on the edge of the Sprigg property, armed with binoculars and a small notebook, sat Jeffrey Bryant. In a darkened third-floor dormer window of the Sprigg house, his own binoculars trained on Jeffrey Bryant, stood Ronnie Sprigg.

"I'm freezing my ass off, Clifford," Duane Minnick shouted. "And I can't see where I'm going. And I'm up to my ass in seaweed or something. Shee-yat."

"Just a little farther, Duane," Clifford said. He was sitting on a large boulder near the end of Sandy Thumb, shouting directions to Duane as Duane waded slowly through the water. It was two in the morning, with no moon, and Duane was only a shivering outline against the sky.

"This is crazy, Clifford!" Duane shouted. "This better not be one of your practical jokes, because this is crazy. This is just plain apeshit crazy."

"About ten more feet, and a little bit to the right, Duane," Clifford shouted. Duane inched ahead. In one hand, he held his clam rake — more or less the way a blind man holds a cane while walking in completely unfamiliar territory. In the other hand, he held the Berryville Runestone.

"Why couldn't we just have left it in the oil pit or

buried it in the backyard, Clifford?" Duane shouted. "He just said to hide it in a safe place, not in a place that would freeze your ass off."

"The last place anybody's going to look for it is where you found it in the first place, Duane. Keep going."

"Shee-yat."

"A couple of feet more, Duane. Hold it. Right there. Get it stuck down in the sand there so it won't drift away."

"It ain't right that losing this goddamned thing is harder than finding it," Duane said, dropping the stone and withdrawing his hand as quickly as possible from the icy water.

"You can come back now, Duane." There was no answer. "Duane?" Clifford peered out into the darkness. He thought he saw the silhouette of Duane Minnick, but then it occurred to him that the silhouette he had taken for Duane might actually be a pine tree on the opposite shore. "Duane!" he shouted. "Are you there, Duane?"

There was a long silence. Then, suddenly, Clifford heard singing coming through the darkness — nasal singing. "I checked over at the Lost & Found when we drifted apart," Duane sang, "to see if someone just by chance had turned in a broken heart."

"Terrible," Clifford said. "That one's just terrible."

George Gustafson, the beer distributor and amateur runologist, arrived in Berryville on a warm July morning three weeks after the Berryville Runestone was discovered, and declared it authentic beyond doubt. The arrival and authentication happened to fall on Jeffrey Bryant's day off, so the story in the *Advance* was written by the reporter who ordinarily spent most of her time covering the meetings of boards that John Sprigg had been elected to. It carried the tone of uncritical acceptance that was commonly used by the *Advance* to report the remarks of the chairman of the United Fund campaign about, say, how much money was saved in administrative costs by consolidating the various charities into one centralized drive. The headline was "Berryville Stone Authenticated."

"Dr. George Gustafson," the story read,

a rune specialist who has published three books on the subject, said yesterday that "the Berryville Runestone is undoubtedly authentic and represents one of the most important archeological discoveries of this century."

Dr. Gustafson, who makes his home in Faribault, Minnesota was in Berryville yesterday to personally inspect the site of the discovery as part of the research he is doing for a book tentatively entitled *Berryville and the Scandinavian Discovery of America*. Dr. Gustafson's previous books include *The Viking Exploration of Long Island, Leif Ericson in Connecticut*, and *The Billings Stone*.

Dr. Gustafson told the *Advance* that the meaning of the inscription on the Berryville Runestone will probably never be known. "That is even further proof of its authenticity," he told the *Advance*. "The eleventh century Scandinavians were the cleverest cryptographers the world has ever known. They were clever in many ways, of course. They had an international-minded ruling class when the court of Spain was still in the hands of Bedouins. They were sending ships around the world at a time when, to take an example, the Italians were squabbling among themselves in mud villages and the Pope was deranged, or perhaps a woman."

The Berryville Runestone has, of course, been missing since shortly after its discovery, but Dr. Gustafson discounted the importance of finding it. He characterized carbon-dating tests as "a flim-flam device used by the nit-pickers."

Dr. Gustafson will be in Berryville until the Runestone Festival, on August 5.

George Gustafson turned out to be a large, stout man who normally wore a blazer displaying the Gustafson family's coat of arms on the breast pocket. His doctorate was honorary, having been awarded by a small Lutheran college in northern Iowa six months after the George Gustafson Library and Archive of Scandinavian Discovery had been built, at a cost to George Gustafson of some three hundred thousand dollars. Arriving in Berryville, Gustafson installed himself in the largest room available at the Berry Vista Motor Lodge — a motel that, under some pressure from John R. Sprigg III, was about to change its name to the Viking Inn. Then he called his press conference in the office of the Chamber of Commerce. Then he sought out Duane Minnick.

Gustafson believed strongly in the principle of Burden of Proof. The burden, in his mind, was completely on the shoulders of those who were out to disprove what he took for granted as an historical certainty — that the Vikings discovered America several hundred years before the voyages of Columbus. Since it was perfectly logical to believe that artifacts of that first Viking exploration would turn up now and then, Gustafson assumed all artifacts to be genuine in the absence of monumental proof to the contrary. The burden of gathering such proof, of course, fell on those people Gustafson normally referred to as "the Columbus fanatics."

Gustafson was particularly delighted by the discovery of the Berryville Runestone, of course, since it was the first one that the professional runologists — "those rigid little moles," as he called them in the preface to *The Billings Stone* — had not dismissed out of hand. He planned to make the Berryville Runestone the central exhibit in his campaign to win the general public's acceptance of Viking primacy. No amount of proof marshaled by the "Columbus fanatics" could alter Gustafson's belief that the Berryville Runestone was what he always called "fundamentally genuine" — meaning that such an artifact obviously existed somewhere in the country, even if the Berryville stone didn't happen to be it. But he knew that the lay public might be sidetracked from the issue of fundamental truth if, for instance, it turned out that the discoverer of the Berryville Runestone, Duane Minnick, had concocted it out of his own imagination and some amateur knowledge of the runic alphabet.

Gustafson found Duane Minnick at Earl's Texaco, under a 1968 Mustang. Clifford Bates was not around, having gone off to the post office to pick up a device that, according to the advertisement, could, if properly hidden in the exhaust pipe of an automobile, give the driver and passengers of that automobile the strong impression that one of their number had very recently stepped in dog feces. Duane, after reflecting momentary disappointment that the imposing visitor in the blue blazer had nothing whatever to do with the music publishing business, was open and unguarded about the discovery. Within a few minutes, Gustafson was satisfied that Duane Minnick was an extremely unlikely participant in any scholarly prank or intellectual hoax. It appeared to Gustafson that Duane Minnick had, as he claimed he had, stumbled onto the Berryville Runestone with no preconceived notions of what it might signify. Gustafson realized that Minnick was, in his own quiet way, a giant of archeology — a man whose relation to the true history of North America was the same as the relation of Schliemann to the true history of Troy.

"Do you, by chance, happen to know what kind of name Minnick is?" he asked Duane.

"What?" Duane said.

"Do you know its origins?"

"What do you mean by that, mister?"

"Its origins," Gustafson repeated. "Is it possible, for instance, that some of your ancestors were, say, Swedish or Danish?"

"No sir. Impossible," Duane said, an uncharacteristic assurance in his voice.

"Are you quite sure?"

"Yes, I sure am," Duane said. "My dad told me our family may have had its share of drinkers, and a couple of people back there might have had some things stick to their fingers that may rightly have belonged to someone down the road. But he said there's one thing we never had, and that's foreigners."

"I'm sorry you feel that way, Milly," Sam Brewster said. He was sitting at his desk in the Berryville Museum, and Millicent Duffrin was hovering over him, shaking a copy of the Berryville *Advance* in his face.

"Here's the proof, Samuel Brewster," she said, throwing the newspaper down on the desk and slapping at it with her hand. "Here is the proof that Sam Brewster is the sort of man who will bend history to suit which side his bread is buttered on. Here is where Sam Brewster, who would never before admit that Berryville was obviously named after berries, is now willing to say so if it supports some concoction about this town being discovered by a gang of European pirates."

Brewster shrugged, and tried to look contrite. He had regretted speculating about the name of the town the moment he read the report of his remarks in the *Advance* and realized that Milly Duffrin must be reading them at the same time. He had regretted it almost daily ever since, as Milly Duffrin stormed into the museum and shook the offending newspaper, now becoming somewhat tattered, in his face. For years, it was true, he had been unwilling to accept a county-wide berry census personally compiled by Milly Duffrin as final proof that Berryville must have been named for its berries. It was understood by everyone in both the Historical Society and the Archeological Society that what drove Millicent Duffrin to spend hours creeping around the thorny scrubbrush of the area searching out new varieties of berries was the persistent legend that the town had not been named for an abundance of berries but for a family named Berry — a family that would have antedated the Duffrins.

"Statistical evidence of a higher count of boysenberries per acre than any county in southern Maine never impressed you a bit, Samuel Brewster," she went on. "But when it comes to making something of an old rock you claimed was scratched by some primitive, then you see berries all over the place."

"Well, Milly —" Sam Brewster began.

"You haven't heard the end of this," Milly Duffrin said.

Brewster shrugged and nodded.

"You're too stubborn to argue with, Sam Brewster," Milly said, and she stamped up the stairs and out of the library.

Jeffrey Bryant was irritated that the *Advance* had blandly accepted the "authentication" of the runestone pronounced by George Gustafson, who, Bryant had gathered from reading *The Billings Stone*, might be capable of pointing to the presence of an abandoned Volvo as proof of early Scandinavian exploration. Bryant decided to mention his concern to Art Norton during their next discussion of the runestone — a regular report to Norton on the progress of the investigation having become more or less routine. From the books he had read on triumphs in investigative reporting, Bryant envisioned long meetings between the reporter and the editor to sort out just what had been learned and what could be proven and which avenues remained to be explored. Norton was a bit phlegmatic to play the role of the editor to perfection — Bryant longed to have his reports met with probing questions and helpful insights rather than with passing wisecracks — but Norton would have to do. The other choice was to go directly to the publisher — Bryant had read about a luncheon meeting between the Washington *Post*'s publisher and its Watergate investigators — but, under the circumstances, a meeting with John R. Sprigg III was obviously inappropriate.

"I don't know if you realized, Mr. Norton, that the 'Doctor' in front of George Gustafson's name doesn't mean he knows anything about Old Norse or pre-Columbian history," Bryant said, at the first meeting he and Norton had after the "authentication."

"Are you saying that the 'Doctor' in front of Frank Trimani's name means he *does* know something about medicine?" Norton asked in reply.

"Well, maybe not, but at least it's not an honorary degree."

"I am pondering on the type of university that might award an honorary degree to Take Two Trimani, and on what the citation might say," Norton said. "Perhaps 'For extensive and courageous research into the universality of two aspirins and prompt billing as a curative.'"

"What I'm getting at, Mr. Norton, is that Gustafson should be on the *Advance*'s list of suspects in this case rather than on its front page as an authority. He's really maniacal on the accomplishments of the medieval Scandinavians."

"I did become slightly suspicious of his views, I must admit, when he implied at the Kiwanis luncheon yesterday that a contemporary of Leif Ericson may have been responsible, indirectly of course, for the invention of the pop-up toaster."

"I thought you might like to be brought up to date on how the list looks," Bryant said. "I've made a chart on who might have been responsible for faking the stone — if it's a fake, of course, which we don't know — or stealing it, if it's been stolen, which, again, we don't know for sure."

"I think that might brighten up my day, Jeffrey," Norton said. "Unless, of course, I am listed among the possible stone-forgers or stone-thieves. On the other hand, being suspected of planting the stone in the water off Sandy Thumb might enhance the meager reputation I have for bravery, since it is widely thought around town that I have never had the nerve to test the temperature of any water saltier than the country club swimming pool until at least the middle of August."

Bryant paused for a while, a look of concentration on his face. "To be perfectly honest, Mr. Norton," he finally said, "I hadn't really thought of you."

"That's quite all right. No offense," Norton said. "Please go on."

"All right. Let us say, first, that the stone was found legitimately by Duane Minnick, that he either left it in the library or took it home with him, and that someone then stole it or suppressed it in some way. And that this someone did it to kill the idea of Berryville as Vinland, not realizing that Duane and Clifford had taken a photograph of the stone — so that stealing it would just give it more publicity instead of leading everyone to assume it hadn't existed in the first place."

"Consider all of that said," Norton said.

Jeffrey withdrew his wallet, extracted from its innermost compartment what appeared to be a tiny piece of paper, and began unfolding it until it became the size of a large poster. "I made a little chart, Mr. Norton," he said. "The kind of people I was just talking about I've listed under the heading 'Possible Stone-Suppressors.'"

"Well, 'stone-suppressor' might have a bit too much of a medical tinge to it if this were the type of thing we had even the remotest notion of putting in the paper," Norton said. "But since we obviously don't, please continue."

"Thank you, Mr. Norton." Bryant spread the chart out on Norton's desk. "One possible stone-suppressor is Gerald Baker Manley," he went on. "I know he visited Lars Kulleseid, who really does know something about Old Norse and pre-Columbian history, because I got there not long after he did. I know he held a meeting of summer people to warn them about how many tourists could be overrunning the place if Berryville does turn out to be Vinland. And I've heard he's become crazier than ever about people coming on to his property. A lawyer I know in Boston told me that, from what all the lawyers are saying down there, Gerald Baker Manley's two acknowledged fields of expertise now are the First

Amendment to the Constitution and the trespass laws of the state of Maine."

Norton nodded. He liked the picture of Gerald Baker Manley sneaking into the backseat of Duane Minnick's Pontiac and nipping off with the stone — or the picture of Gerald Baker Manley emerging from his hiding place in the men's room of the library after everyone had left for the day, grabbing the stone, and walking out with regular library patrons when the building was opened up the following morning, after an evening spent sleeping on the dusty carpet of the Science & Technology section.

"Next, I have Millicent Duffrin," Bryant said.

"Milly Duffrin!"

"Yes sir. I'm afraid you'd have to put her name on any list of potential stone-suppressors. Doesn't it seem strange to you, for instance, that not a word on all of this has been heard from the Berryville Historical Society? Millicent Duffrin, of course, controls the Berryville Historical Society, and, as everyone knows, is practically obsessed with proving beyond any doubt that the most important historical event in Berryville's history was the arrival of the Duffrins before everyone else. What if Leif Ericson beat the Duffrins here by six or seven hundred years? There aren't any Ericsons around to be the oldest family, of course, but if this really was Vinland nobody is going to pay much attention to colonial history around here any more."

Norton smiled, having found the vision of Milly Duffrin snatching the stone from Duane's car even more entertaining than the one of Gerald Baker Manley hiding in the library men's room.

"She needn't have physically swiped it, of course," Bryant said. "She could have persuaded Duane, through some bribe, to lose it. I say persuaded Duane because if the stone was really left in the library, she could have never got very far with Sam Brewster. He was much too interested in authenticating the stone. In fact, he's on my list of possible stone-concocters. It would guarantee his spot in the history of archeology and it would blow Milly Duffrin and her colonial history business out of the water. Also, of course, he was in a position to both concoct the stone and to make it disappear before it could be thoroughly studied. Except Kulleseid tells me that if anyone concocted the stone, that person knew an awful lot about runology. I think Mr. Brewster would have tried to handle something like that himself — being proud of his archeological knowledge, and all — and I guess I think he probably couldn't have handled it. I understand he found a microwave oven once and thought it belonged to the Indians, although I haven't checked that out."

"It was a hibachi," Norton said. "But the principle's the same."

"I'm keeping him on the list anyway, of course," Bryant said.

"I take it, though, that the number one suspect remains the man I think I can describe in a nutshell as the person who signs our paychecks and can fire us on the tiniest whim."

"I'm afraid so, Mr. Norton," Bryant said. "And I'm afraid he just might be in danger."

"If you mean from Milly Duffrin," Norton said, "she might rough him up a bit, but I doubt that she would do him any permanent damage."

"No sir, I don't mean Milly Duffrin. I mean The Mob."

"Could you have possibly said 'The Mob'?"

"Yes sir, I'm afraid so."

"By that you mean organized crime, the syndicate, Cosa Nostra, the Mafia, the Black Hand — that sort of organization?"

"I know it seems unlikely in Berryville," Bryant said. "But I think we have reason to believe they're interested in this. Yesterday, a Mr. Vincent Lucelli of Lodi, New Jersey, registered at the Viking Inn. On the part of the registration card that asked what organization he represented he wrote Italian-American Historical Preservation Society. Well, I thought I had heard of that group, so I went to the library and looked it up in the *New York Times* index, and then I went through the microfilm of the *Times*."

"This is all very intrepid of you so far, Jeffrey," Norton said. "Especially the part about the registration card."

"Thank you, Mr. Norton. Anyway, according to some

stories in the *Times,* the only historical event the Italian-American Historical Preservation Society is much interested in preserving is the discovery of America by Christopher Columbus. One story said that when a professor at Rutgers published a book a few years ago claiming that it was more likely that Columbus was a Jewish Marrano rather than an Italian, a couple of bricks were thrown through the professor's front window. The I.A.H.P.S. was apparently suspected, and they never did exactly flatly deny it."

"Let me get this straight," Norton said. "If it turns out that Johnny-Three did have the stone concocted, the mob will lean on him because he had promoted Leif Ericson at the expense of Christopher Columbus?"

"That's right," Bryant said, quickly folding up his chart as he noticed another reporter wandering over toward Norton's desk.

"Well, well," Norton said. "I believe that's the kind of thing Johnny-Three would call 'downbeat stuff.' Interesting, but definitely downbeat stuff."

Lawrence I. DiCarlo was in such a rush when he came into the Yankee Cafe that he stood as he waited for his coffee. Heather Palermo was supposed to be covering the counter while Mike Derounian went through some bills, but Derounian could see that Heather had become too engrossed in adjusting one of her eyelashes to notice the mayor. Derounian took the coffee over himself, put it on the counter in front of the mayor, and said, "Morning, Larry."

"Yeah," the mayor replied, glancing toward the door. "Lot to do."

"Look, Larry," Derounian said. "If the water keeps coming through I'm afraid it might short out the juke-box."

"Jesus Christ, Mike!" DiCarlo said. "How can you talk to me about leaks at a time like this? Everyone keeps calling me to say that mobster friend of Christopher Columbus is still in town. Jeffrey Bryant wrote in the *Advance* today that someone hired LEPKO, that high-powered goddamned research outfit, to investigate the stone. I was down to the police station already this morning talking to Max Hebert, and he tells me that loony Swede Gustafson's got half the Canucks in this town mad enough to kill someone by telling them all they may really be Danish or some damn thing. And Johnny-Three tells me I'm going to have to write a speech presenting the first Distinguished Viking award to that little shit-hook Duane Minnick. What are you talking to me about leaks?"

"I'm sorry, Larry," Derounian said. "You do look kind of harassed."

"It's O.K.," DiCarlo said. "Skip it."

"Is all that Italian stuff bothering you, Larry?" Derounian asked.

"What Italian stuff?"

"You know, Larry. The stuff about Italians being downgraded because we're saying the Swedes or whoever the hell they were came here first. I mean, you being Italian yourself and all."

DiCarlo looked at his watch, and then sat down. "I've thought about it a lot, Mike," he said. "Believe me, I've thought about it. I've looked at it from a lot of angles — a lot of angles. Let's just say, for instance, I'm thinking about myself strictly — O.K.?"

"O.K., Larry," Derounian said.

"Well, then, what this means is that the Italians are less important, but it means that Berryville is more important. And I'm Italian but I'm also the mayor of Berryville, so that makes the Italians more important again. Also, it makes me more important, if I do say so myself."

"I guess so, Larry. Sure."

"But I'm trying to think about the town, Mike. I really am. I was thinking about everything last night, and I thought, well, the only things I really want that I don't have is to get some decent economic base for this town and to get some way to build that water-treatment plant and to find out who the hell Heather Palermo is with when she calls in sick. Then I'd be a happy man."

"I know what you mean, Larry," Derounian said.

"Also, we're all Americans," DiCarlo said. "Even that little pissant Duane Minnick is an American, for Christ's sake. It's hard to believe, but he is. It really doesn't make that much difference who was here first."

"I guess you're right," Derounian said. "I don't really care who was here first. Unless, of course, it was the Turks. Jesus, I do hate those Turks. There's no Armenian that doesn't hate the Turks. But I never heard anybody claim it was the Turks, so I couldn't care less. I don't know. I guess this is all good for the town, but Johnny-Three has such a bug up his ass about it he's about to drive us all nuts. He was in here yesterday morning wanting me to change the name of this place to 'Leif's Lair' or something. I told him if we ever started serving moose steak on a regular basis, we'd call it 'Leif's Lair.' "

Henry LaDoux slipped into the seat next to DiCarlo. "How about 'Leif's Leaky Lair?' " he said.

DiCarlo frowned, and looked at his watch. "Hiya, Henry," he said. "I gotta go." He stood up, and started sipping rapidly at his coffee.

"Larry's going to have to write a speech so he can present Duane Minnick with the first Distinguished Viking award at the festival," Derounian said to LaDoux.

"I guess you're fresh out of Distinguished Moron awards and that's why you're giving him a Distinguished Viking award," LaDoux said.

"Well, he did find the goddamned thing," DiCarlo

said. "And Johnny-Three thinks if people see him up on the platform nobody is going to get any ideas that the guy who found it is any kind of shrewd forger or anything."

"Does the kid know he's going to be getting an award?" LaDoux asked.

"Yeah, he said he's scared to death to speak in public and asked if he could sing a song instead," DiCarlo said. "We told him if he knew a song in Old Norse he could sing a song. Otherwise, he would make a nice short thank-you speech and get his ass off the platform."

"Bertha Winstead tells me the Historical Society may pass a resolution against the festival," LaDoux said to DiCarlo.

"Don't talk to me about the Historical Society," Di-Carlo said. "A bunch of Yankee faggots is what they are as far as I'm concerned. They're all scared to death of Milly Duffrin. She came up to me on the street yesterday and asked me what authority I had to spend public funds on celebrating 'some primitive sailors.' "

"Speaking of being scared to death, what's with the mobster these days?" Derounian asked.

"As far as I know, he hasn't talked to anyone since he came into town," DiCarlo said. "To tell you the truth, I've been so busy figuring out who to invite to watch the parade from the reviewing stand and what the order of the parade should be and making sure the Jaycees won't

screw up as usual on ordering the clams for the clambake I haven't had time to worry about the son of a
bitch. If he bumps off that loony Swede I take back
anything nasty I ever said about the mob."

"Maybe you can have the reviewing stand in front of
the pothole, Larry," LaDoux said. "That way, you can be
sure everyone slows up in front of the distinguished
guests. Of course, you might lose a drum majorette or
two in there — or maybe a small drum and bugle corps."

"As a matter of fact, smartass, that's just where the
reviewing stand is going to be," DiCarlo said. "Johnny-
Three told me on the q.t. he's ninety percent sure CBS or
ABC is going to cover the parade, and if they do they're
going to have one of their crews fix the pothole once and
for all just to make sure nothing happens in front of the
camera."

"Well, one thing good is going to come out of the stone
anyway," LaDoux said. "If that pothole gets fixed by
someone more competent than those clowns in the city
crew, Duane Minnick is a Distinguished Viking in my
book."

"You're right," Derounian said. "Now all we have to do
is see if we can get NBC to fix the roof."

LEPKO — a research and consulting firm known by
an acronym whose origin no one seemed to remember —
had, in theory, been hired by the Institute of New En-

gland Culture, a cooperative venture of six Boston-area universities, to do a report on "the background, authenticity, and cultural implications of the so-called Berryville Runestone." But one of the most influential trustees of the Institute of New England Culture was Gerald Baker Manley, and Mayor DiCarlo had no doubt that LEPKO's investigation was part of an attempt by Manley to prove the stone fraudulent. LEPKO was, as it happened, the same firm that had once been hired by Berryville and two nearby cities to investigate the feasibility of a joint water-treatment plant — a project that was inspired by some slightly inaccurate information given to Mayor DiCarlo about the availability of grants under a regional cooperation title in the 1967 Urban and Regional Development Act — as well as the firm once hired by the Berryville City Council to prepare a report on whether Berryville should invest bond money into converting the old tractor-gear factory into a convention center.

The three researchers who had been assigned to the runestone inquiry by LEPKO established headquarters at the Viking Inn, and began interviewing everyone involved in the discovery — Duane Minnick, Clifford Bates, Sam Brewster, even Bertha Winstead. They spent hours off Sandy Thumb, doing water-temperature tests and tide charts. They gathered data for a number of color-coordinated overlay charts they were planning to prepare — a chart, for instance, showing the distances between the alleged runestones found in the United States in each decade, and a chart showing, through vertical and horizontal hash marks, the incidence of stone-discovery by state in correlation to national-origin figures on the United States census tracts.

From the porch of his summer house, Gerald Baker Manley sometimes watched the LEPKO researchers through his telescope as they poked around in the water off Sandy Thumb — a couple of them taking measurements, another one writing everything down on a clipboard. Having read a number of LEPKO studies in the past, Manley suspected that any useful information in the runestone report would prove to be, on careful examination, indistinguishable from the information already presented in the water-treatment plant report and the convention-center report. He had little faith in LEPKO ever coming up with anything except a stunning variety of charts. But he believed that the desperation of the situation called for the use of any weapons available, no matter how unlikely their effectiveness.

For some time after Leah Rifkind's outburst about the rock's attracting blacks to Berryville, the summer people, disturbed at being cast in the role of racists or elitists, had been reluctant even to organize themselves into a group to look into the potential impact of the stone discovery. But the announcement that the Chamber of Commerce's Promotion and Development Committee had recommended the acquisition of Sandy Thumb for use as a theme-park spread panic among them. The Sandy Thumb Environmental Task Force was organized. Within two weeks it had distributed press releases demanding an environmental impact study before any development took place, quoting a marine biologist on the danger any development would present to clam life in the Sandy Thumb area, and describing, in some detail, the place of the clam in the ecostructure of the northeastern coast of the United States.

Manley, though, knew that the Sandy Thumb Environmental Task Force could provide merely a holding action if the stone were accepted as authentic and the city managed to acquire Sandy Thumb from whichever tangle of heirs was found to be its owner. The summer people, after all, did not vote in Berryville, and the local businessmen seemed united in the belief that the rock could serve as a magical tool for prying loose millions of dollars' worth of easy tourist money for the town. Manley had begun to have bad dreams of Berryville as Vinland. In his dreams, the storefronts on Main Street — now so nondescript and in keeping with the architecture of the nineteenth-century tractor-gear factory — had been transformed into an ersatz Scandinavian village by the addition of the facades that in other parts of the country passed as Swiss or Bavarian, depending on which sort of cheap-import souvenirs were for sale. Mayor DiCarlo strutted up and down the street, wearing one of the fur hats with horns that Vikings in the films always wear, toasting mobs of tourists with an overflowing flagon of beer. In Sandy Thumb, that idyllic spot Manley had so longed to own, the theme-park had been erected. Loudly dressed day-trippers swarmed all over what had once been picturesque beaches. They ate grotesquely outsized cones of soft ice cream. They threw beer cans at the surf. They wore huge Viking hats, with their names sewn on them in script. When Manley had the dream, he always felt himself trying to get away from the noise and lights of the park — trying to recapture the peaceful, country-house sleep he had luxuriated in before the stone was discovered. But the park in his dream would stay open long into the night — the tourists screaming as they swooped down on Viking-boat roller coasters or were jarred around in Viking-boat bumper cars. Even when the tourists had departed at last, sleep was impossible because the Scandinavian beer companies, competing for customers in the most appropriate North American setting they had ever found, kept their huge neon signs flashing all night. The quiet darkness that used to envelop his house was, in his dream, broken with flashing neon: TUBORG, CARLSBERG. TUBORG, CARLSBERG. TUBORG, CARLSBERG.

All of the various people who had come to Berryville to look into the discovery of the Berryville Runestone were staying at the Viking Inn, but they had little to say to each other about the stone. They nodded at each other while waiting to be seated in the Viking Inn's restaurant, and passed an occasional remark about the weather, and kept their own counsel. Vincent Lucelli, as far as anyone could make out, had hardly uttered a word since his arrival in Berryville. It was rumored that he had been seen chatting with Guido Popolizio, but, even assuming the truth of the rumor, nobody would have known what they said to each other, since Popolizio spoke only a Genoese dialect that even the Italians in Berryville found incomprehensible. Lucelli spent much of his time walking up and down the main street of Berryville, occasionally nodding solemnly at the storekeepers — all of whom were scrutinizing him to discover where he might be carrying what kind of weapon. "He's just trying to look sinister, of course," Art Norton said to the gathering at the Yankee Cafe one morning. "And, with all that experience, he's quite good at it by now." Lucelli was a tall, slim, unsmiling man, with a sallow complexion. He was always dressed in a brown suit that seemed slightly too large for him. Every day at low tide, he would walk to Sandy Thumb, picking his way along the rocks in his pointed city shoes as far as he could go without stepping in the water, studying the area fifteen or twenty yards away, where Duane Minnick was said to have found the stone.

George Gustafson also walked daily along the beach near Sandy Thumb, occasionally passing Lucelli, with whom he would exchange silent, unsmiling nods. Gustafson was not troubled by Lucelli's silence. He made it a habit not to talk to Italians unless absolutely necessary, on the grounds that just about all of them were, as he often put it, "living the lie of Columbus." Gustafson was looking for landscapes that would match the descriptions in *Karlsefni's Saga* and some of the other accounts of Viking voyages. He was confident he could find a significant amount of matching topography; he had never experienced any real difficulty finding matching topography, even in Montana.

At dinner in the motel restaurant, there were always three or four separate tables occupied by rune investigators of one sort of another — the LEPKO researchers, Gustafson, Lucelli, a man from the state Parks & Culture Department who visited regularly for a report he was preparing, an occasional out-of-town journalist. Jeffrey Bryant often came in at dinnertime to table-hop — picking up a bit of runic lore here, exchanging a confidence about local citizens there, nodding silently to Lucelli on the way out. Since he had decided that the key fact in the runestone mystery might be who stood to profit from an increase in the value of Sandy Thumb, Bryant spent most of his spare time at the county deeds office, trying to untangle the ownership. He had, by his estimate, purchased at least twenty-five cups of bad coffee for a particularly unattractive and unpleasant secretary who was rumored to be skilled in facilitating the recovery of files buried somewhere in the county courthouse annex's sub-basement. But he was always on the alert to pick up information on other angles of the story. Off the record, some of the investigators were occasionally open about their suspicions — particularly the state Parks & Culture man, who seemed certain that Clifford Bates had been involved somehow.

"I just don't think Clifford would be up to faking runic inscriptions," Bryant told the Parks & Culture man one evening.

"He's more sophisticated than you think," the Parks & Culture man said. "Did you know he once had a dog he named Full Frontal Nudity?"

"I didn't know that," Bryant said. "But there's a long way between naming a dog Full Frontal Nudity and learning Old Norse well enough to fool Lars Kulleseid."

"Maybe so," the Parks & Culture man said. "But somebody did it. Berryville just can't be Vinland. Berryville doesn't even have a radio station. It just doesn't make sense."

As usual, the Spriggs sat down to dinner at seven, and, as usual, not much of the meal had passed before Claudia Sprigg had to kick her husband under the table to remind him not to lose his temper at their son. As usual, Ronnie Sprigg had been polite from the start.

"You haven't really told me what you think about the runestone, Ronnie," John R. Sprigg III said as soup was being served.

"I'm terribly sorry, Dad," Ronnie said, sounding genuinely concerned. "I didn't realize you wanted to know." He went on eating his soup. For a minute or two there was silence.

"Yes," Sprigg finally said, "I did want to know."

"Well," Ronnie said. "I do think that the discovery of what might be a genuine Viking artifact on the coast of Maine is potentially an interesting event."

There was another long silence. "Ronnie," John Sprigg finally said. "I hope you're not one of those ecology lunatics who hate the idea of any progress if it's going to spoil a perch for one pigeon."

"I love a cold soup in the summer — don't you, John?" Mrs. Sprigg said.

"Thank you, Dad. It's nice of you to be concerned," Ronnie said, in his usual pleasant voice. "Lunacy would certainly be a cross to bear these days."

"What I was hoping, actually," Sprigg said, "was that you might be interested in taking a hand in the preparations for the Runestone Festival. It seems to me that it would be right up your alley, with your course in archeology and all."

"Thanks a lot, Dad," Ronnie said. "It's nice of you to

think of it. Unfortunately, I'm rather busy these days."

"Busy?"

"Yes, sir."

"Anything I can help with?" John Sprigg said.

"Oh, no thanks, Dad. It's just investments — that sort of thing."

There was another long silence. John R. Sprigg III began to grow flushed. Claudia Sprigg kicked him under the table. She had hoped that someday she and her husband and their son would be able to make it through an entire dinner without the necessity of a kick, but the soup course remained her record.

The regular meeting of the Berryville Historical Society, held at the Berryville Free Library, had drawn five or six times its usual attendance — the word having been passed around town that a vote on the Runestone Festival would be on the meeting's agenda. Many Berryville residents whose membership in the historical society had been nominal in the past were at the library before the appointed time — including Sam Brewster and a number of other people whose more active membership was in the Berryville Archeological Society, which had already gone on record as a strong supporter of the Berryville Runestone. At precisely eight o'clock, the time the meeting had been scheduled to begin, Millicent Duffrin walked in with Vincent Lucelli.

Milly Duffrin had a knowing smile on her face as she

opened the meeting. "We certainly welcome the sudden interest of many of you in your area's history," she said. "It is gratifying to all of us to have an attendance of this sort, particularly at a time when our town is going through a period during which sober, analytical, objective historical analysis — as opposed to, for instance, eagerness to accept any unsubstantiated and outlandish historical claim that might suit our pocketbooks — is so sorely needed. I'm certain, in that sense, all of us will have much to gain from listening to our guest speaker, Professor Vincent Lucelli."

Vincent Lucelli's silence, it turned out, had not been due to any lack of facility with the language — which came as no surprise to his listeners after they had learned, in Milly Duffrin's introduction, that he was a graduate of the University of Padua and Trinity College, Cambridge, a Ph.D. in history from Stanford University, and a fellow in fifteenth- and sixteenth-century history at the University of Salamanca, as well as a visiting lecturer at universities in Zurich and Lyon and chief historical consultant to the Italian-American Historical Preservation Society. His speech to the Berryville Historical Society — a shortened version, he explained, of the new introduction he had prepared for a French edition of his book on fifteenth-century European exploration — was remarkable for its clarity and its wit and its subtle but unmistakable allusions to primary source material. As

Lucelli spoke, the court of Ferdinand and Isabella seemed to come alive — the ambitious Spanish monarchs, the earnest Italian navigator possessed with the need to demonstrate that his theory on a route to the Indies was correct. At the conclusion of the speech, most of those in the audience rose to their feet in applause. Professor Lucelli smiled, rather shyly. "I would, naturally, be happy to answer any questions that you or your colleagues have, Miss Duffrin," he said.

There was an uneasy silence, and then Sam Brewster, having been nudged repeatedly by the Chamber of Commerce board members sitting on either side of him, raised his hand. "I hate to bring this up, Professor," Brewster said. "But I don't think it's any secret around town that the organization you represent — I don't mean the University of Salamanca or Cambridge or anything; I mean the Italian-American organization — has a reputation for, well, you know, rough stuff. No offense meant, you understand."

"No offense taken, of course, Mr. Brewster," Lucelli said. "I'm grateful to you for bringing up this matter. As you can see, I'm a harmless enough fellow myself." He paused and smiled, and most people in the audience chuckled. "As a scholar, I would, of course, deplore violence or intimidation in scholarly arguments," he continued. "As I'm sure you know from your own extensive research, Mr. Brewster, people do become rather headstrong when they believe they are in possession of an objective truth that is being challenged or suppressed for some nonscholarly reason. This may be said of Galileo, for instance, if you'll forgive me for bringing up the name of another one of my countrymen."

It was partly because of the impression made by Lucelli in his speech and his answers to the questions of Brewster and others that, despite the presence of a number of people other than those who routinely followed Milly Duffrin's lead, she was able to put through a resolution stating that the Berryville Historical Society would have no part in "any attempt to substitute for painstaking and scholarly historical research the false history dictated by commercial considerations." It was a way of saying, everyone realized, that the historical society would not participate in the Berryville Runestone Festival. As the entire resolution was worded, in fact, it kept open the possibility that the historical society might picket the Berryville Runestone Festival.

Two days before the Runestone Festival, Larry Di-Carlo was, as Art Norton put it, "in a state of suspended exasperation." DiCarlo could hardly stay in one place long enough to complete a sentence, but even in fragments and subsidiary clauses he managed to express his outrage at the forces that seemed to be conspiring to ruin the best opportunity Berryville ever had. Despite entreaties from the Chamber of Commerce and the mayor and John R. Sprigg III, the Historical Society had been implacable in its opposition to the festival; Milly Duffrin had been seen emerging from Roy Bouchard's hobby shop carrying an armload of white cardboard that looked suitable for use as placards. Duane Minnick had been almost equally stubborn about singing during the ceremony if he appeared at all. Finally, at John Sprigg's suggestion, DiCarlo offered Duane the opportunity to choose the Viking Princess in exchange for a promise to accept the award with a simple, nonmusical thank-you. Duane accepted the offer, and chose Myrna McDonald, known to everybody in Berryville as "the town pump."

"I know that smartass Clifford Bates put him up to it," DiCarlo almost shouted to Mike Derounian as he gulped down an early-morning cup of coffee — standing at the counter while his pickup stood with its motor running right outside the door. "I should have that little bastard arrested. I know we could get him on that business with the Up Yours signs if we grilled him in the back of the police station for a couple of days. Gotta go."

"Calm down, Larry," Derounian said. "Take it easy. Have a seat. None of the outsiders know Myrna's got hinged heels." With forty-eight hours to go, DiCarlo was already red in the face, and Derounian, concerned about the mayor's health, had pledged himself not to mention the Yankee Cafe's leaking roof until after the festival was over.

DiCarlo sat down. Derounian poured him another cup of coffee. "You know, LaDoux and Marchetti are starting to keep a chart on which days Heather calls in sick, so they can see who else around town turns up missing those days," Derounian said, trying to switch the subject from the Runestone Festival. "How do you like the way she looks in that new waitress uniform?"

"In my condition, I'm afraid to look," DiCarlo said. "Did you know the goddamned Jaycees can't find enough clams for the clambake? I know they're going to run out of clams and then the goddamned environmentalists are going to say, 'See, you're threatening the clam population of the eastern seaboard.' The miserable goddamned clam is supposed to be an endangered species or something."

"Don't worry, Larry," Derounian said. "There's nothing to worry about from the environmentalists. I hear they decided not to picket." The Sandy Thumb Environmental Task Force had, in fact, come to a decision not to picket, after a bitter debate on the subject during which Porter Fox called Andrea Fenton, the leader of those who thought picketing might be counterproductive, a "fascist collaborator."

"I was up half the night trying to convince this dumb grant-officer from HUD that the law doesn't say a town has to be full of Navajos or something to be 'culturally impacted,'" DiCarlo said. "Christ knows what the loony Swede is up to. He signed up for a float in the parade under the name of the Scandinavian historical something or other. For all I know, it'll show Leif Ericson inventing color T.V. in his spare time. The stupid damn printer for the *Advance* supplement, which is only supposed to be the program for the whole goddamned festival, spelled 'rune' like 'ruin' right straight through, so the thing had to be sent back and it may not be ready in time. I wake up in the middle of the night all the time thinking the agency — the one in Washington — has just called me and said the stone says something like 'Get your winter tune-up at Earl's Texaco.' Gotta go."

At the suggestion of John R. Sprigg III, the Runestone Festival's publicity committee tried to steer any visiting reporters who had questions about the discovery of the stone toward Sam Brewster — Sprigg's theory being that a short appearance by Duane Minnick on the award platform would be quite enough exposure of the stone's discoverer for anybody. But Maxine Thomas, the Boston television interviewer, would not be sidetracked. Her program, "Maxine Thomas Live," had a reputation for being the most direct, probing, provocative interview program on television. She always worked live rather than on tape or film, and always asked questions that ranged from provocative to insulting. She often referred to herself as being on "the cutting edge of journalism." Ignoring hints that Sam Brewster might be the man to talk to about the details of the runestone discovery, she did her show live from Earl's Texaco, opening up by asking Duane Minnick if he had faked the discovery of a runestone to put his name before the public as a country singer and composer.

"No, ma'am," Duane said. Maxine Thomas had whipped her microphone out of her purse so quickly that Duane was almost too stunned to be frightened.

"And your latest song isn't about a lost and found?" she pressed.

"No, ma'am" said Duane, who had written at least fifteen songs since the one about a lost and found. "My latest song is 'It's True the Coveralls I Wear Are Green, but I'm the Bluest Car Mechanic You Have Ever Seen.' Would you like to hear it?"

Maxine Thomas had even worse luck with Clifford, as she probed for what his angle might be in the discovery. "What are you into, Clifford?" she said, shoving her microphone close to his face.

"Nothing, really."

"Oh, come on. What's your thing?"

"I don't really have one," Clifford said.

"You must have a thing, Clifford."

"No I don't," Clifford said. "It was shot off in the war."

There was a long pause. Clifford stood with a serious expression, patiently waiting for the next question, but, for the first time on live television, Maxine Thomas didn't seem to have another question to ask. "Oh," she finally managed.

"So I'm really not into anything, if you get my meaning," Clifford said.

"Oh," Maxine Thomas repeated. "I'm terribly sorry." Clifford shrugged, and looked at the ground, and kicked at the dirt.

The special-events crew that was setting up to film the parade and festival as part of the "Out There in America" series was much less interested in getting to the heart of the matter. Its director, in fact, had met with John R. Sprigg III and the chairman of the parade committee and Mayor DiCarlo to talk about ways to shoot around any demonstrators who might appear to mar the festivities.

"We certainly do appreciate your cooperation," Sprigg said. "And your boys did a bang-up job on the pothole."

"No problem," the director said. "Listen, this is such a relief after five years of doing the Columbus Day parade in New York — all those fat, overdressed guineas marching down the middle of . . . oh, sorry, Mayor, no offense."

DiCarlo shrugged. "Just a figure of speech," the director went on.

"Don't worry, don't worry," John Sprigg said. "We're all Vikings here."

On the afternoon before the Runestone Festival, everyone in Berryville seemed to have adopted Mayor DiCarlo's pace. The television crew from "Out There in America" was running huge cables back and forth across the street for the parade coverage. Some city workers were stringing purple banners along the second floor of the Main Street storefronts. Roy Bouchard was supervising two men who were removing the plate glass window of his hobby shop preparatory to building an open-air counter for selling stones and film and beer. The Berryville High School Roarin' Redskins Marching Band was having its final rehearsal — the drum majorettes still in their traditional headbands and fringed hot pants, an effort by John R. Sprigg III to have the name of the school's teams and band changed from Indians to Vikings in time for the festival having been resisted successfully by the alumni association. Myrna McDonald and Betty Lu Mosher, a friend who worked at the Berry Hair Boutique, were trying to work out a way to achieve the Viking effect in a hairdo for Myrna to wear as Viking Princess. Sam Brewster was taking two Boston reporters on a long tour of the Museum's arrowhead and pot collection. Several Jaycees were gathered around the chairman of the clambake committee as he desperately phoned sea food distributors as far away as New York trying to find some more clams. DiCarlo himself was constantly leaping in and out of his pickup truck — encouraging, directing, complaining about what had gone wrong at the previous stop. Milly Duffrin — supplied with good stiff cardboard, stencils, and marking pens — was supervising a group of her hard-core followers as they prepared picket signs.

In the garage at Earl's Texaco, Duane Minnick and Clifford Bates sat on the runners above the grease rack talking about Duane's appearance the next day to receive the first Distinguished Viking award. When Duane agreed not to sing, he hadn't realized how much he truly dreaded having to say even a few words of thank-you — without a tune, without an imaginary guitar to thwack-thwack, without the protection of that nasal monotone that turned him into a loose and casual good old boy who had just drifted in from Nashville. "I can't do it, Clifford," Duane said. "I can't get up in front of all those people and say anything. I'll forget what I'm supposed to say. I'm scared shitless, Clifford."

"You can write out what you're going to say, Duane," Clifford said. "You can just read some nice humble speech like 'It sure is great that this first Distinguished Viking award went to an ordinary little shithead like me.'"

"Come on, Clifford, you've got to help me."

"I offered to write you a little speech and help you practice it, Duane. I even offered to carve it on a rock if you think that'd be cute."

"I couldn't stand to practice it," Duane said. "That would make it worse when I got up there. I'd know where I was going to make mistakes from before."

"I'll tell you what, Duane. I'll write a speech, a very short speech, and give it to you just before you go up to the microphone."

"Yeah, Clifford?"

"Right. Then you just pull it out of your pants and read it, just like reading a letter for the first time. You might even get so you work up some interest in hearing what you're about to say."

"Could you do that really, Clifford?"

"Sure, Duane."

"Clifford?"

"Yeah, Duane."

"Short words, O.K.?"

"Little bitty ones, Duane."

"It's remarkably peaceful in here, Mr. Jones," Ronnie Sprigg was saying. They were sitting in their accustomed booth toward the rear of Wong's Garden of the Orient. Ronnie Sprigg was finishing off a plate of crab with ginger and scallions. Alonzo Jones was watching with some gratification.

"I believe the Orient is known for its serenity," Jones said, "although I hasten to say that I do not speak from personal experience."

"And for its cuisine," Ronnie said.

"I'm pleased that you find it to your liking, Mr. Sprigg."

"Outside of this peaceful oasis, I must say, everyone in Berryville seems as busy as could be today, Mr. Jones. Has it occurred to you that the discovery of the stone has been good for the town's spirit as well as for its commerce? I think it's fair to say that a sense of pride that was not previously present can be identified."

"Well, living in Vinland is no small matter, Mr. Sprigg," Jones said. "Particularly for people who had previously lived merely in the heart of the Yankee shore."

"It's rather interesting to see how quickly the residents seem to take on their role as the inheritors of the Viking tradition," Sprigg said. "Did you happen to see the Channel 3 news from Portland last night, Mr. Jones?"

"I'm afraid six-thirty is our busiest time for dispensing egg rolls and chow mein to the local gourmets," Jones said.

"Of course. I forgot. Well, Channel 3 news opened with a shot of Guido Popolizio whittling."

"How is that new santo of his coming?" Jones asked. "I've been meaning to drop by some afternoon to take a look at it. I must say, though, that my attempts to master that Genoese dialect have not been very successful, and old Guido and I are almost reduced to sign language."

"The santo is coming slowly, I'm afraid," Sprigg said. "It has occurred to me, now and then, that Guido may not be able to whittle awfully well. I realized the other day that I have never known him to complete anything. At any rate, there he was on the television set, carving away, and the voice-over was saying something like 'Recognize the wind-seamed face, the strong hands, the steady gaze? They may be the same kind of wind-seamed face, strong hands, and steady gaze possessed by the legendary Vikings — perhaps the forebears of this old whittler.'"

"Yes, old Guido does almost as well as a Viking as he did as a Yankee," Jones said. "An interesting minor irony, of course, is that, being Genoese, he could actually claim that one of his forebears was not John Alden or Leif Ericson but Christopher Columbus."

"A good point, Mr. Jones," Sprigg said. "And may I ask you how you're able to put your hands on crabs of this quality?"

"Supplier, Mr. Sprigg," Jones said. "Merely a matter of finding the right supplier. At any rate, what you say about old Guido brings up a point we have discussed before: it doesn't really make much difference whether or not racial and ethnic myths are true. Guido can be a symbol of Viking adventure just as legitimately as he was a symbol of Yankee independence — and all without speaking a word of English or, needless to say, Old Norse. The same principle holds for Mayor DiCarlo — formerly the proudest member of the Colonial Drum & Bugle Corps, now the leader of the oldest Viking settlement in the New World. The mayor always had a bit of a problem with Yankee taciturnity, of course, but I think that most of the French-Canadian and Italian and Irish and Jewish businessmen along Main Street made fine Yankees during our Yankee period. I wouldn't be surprised if they started behaving more like Scandinavians before long, if they can figure out what Scandinavians behave like."

"Or maybe like the subjects of the Pharaoh Necho," Sprigg said.

"Well, they say anything is possible in America, Mr. Sprigg," Jones said.

On the morning of the first Berryville Runestone Festival, Mayor DiCarlo was at the Yankee Cafe by seven, but he was in such a rush that he seemed torn between walking toward the counter and bolting back toward the door. "It isn't even raining," he said. "No rain. I would have bet anything it would rain. God's the only one not trying to screw this whole thing up right in front of my eyes, because the only thing it's not is raining."

"I noticed it wasn't raining, Larry," Derounian said.

"I'm usually the first person inside to find out if it's raining, if you know what I mean." Derounian immediately regretted having brought up his leaking roof, but the mayor had been too excited to notice anyway.

"I got to get over to the park to check on the Jaycees right now," DiCarlo said, still standing between the counter and the door. "They've screwed up, as usual. The future leading executives of the whole goddamn world they're supposed to be, and they can't find clams on the coast of Maine. I bet the Jaycees in the middle of Iowa can't figure out how to get their hands on any corn. All the flags the parade committee ordered turned out to be Swiss instead of Swedish, and Sam Brewster says the Vikings were more like Norwegians than Swedes anyway. The crazy son of a bitch Gustafson almost blew out of his blazer when he saw the flags. He says the Swiss don't even have any ocean ports and never made ships and can't swim and Christ knows what all. I don't know. Give me a quick cup of coffee, Mike; I only got a second. Anyway, the supplement or the program or whatever the hell it's called is finally out and they spelled 'rune' right. Of course everything else is spelled wrong. I'm surprised sometimes that they spell the name of the town right when they say 'The Berryville *Advance*' there on the front page. I think when Johnny-Three finds a reporter over there who can spell cat he switches him to the business department and chains him to an adding machine. I got to run, Mike. The stupid bastards in charge of the tourist information stands dressed all the girls in those old colonial costumes they used to wear on the Fourth of July when we were still the Heart of the goddamn Yankee Shore. The parade is probably a mess. Jesus!"

The mayor half-trotted out the door, leaving his coffee on the counter untouched. He leaped into his pickup truck and drove to the Little League field, where the floats and bands of the parade were forming a line of march. There had been some difference of opinion in town about whether, under the circumstances, it would be appropriate for Berryville's Colonial Drum & Bugle Corps to take its traditional place at the head of the parade. The issue had finally been settled, more or less by default, when it became apparent that may of the members of the Drum & Bugle Corps were going to be occupied overseeing the parade or arranging the ceremonies that were to follow it or tending to their own business ventures in anticipation of thousands of tourists — an expert from the state Tourist Commission having estimated that the number of people who might ordinarily be expected to come to Berryville to watch a parade and Runestone Festival would have to be doubled considering the number of people who would come to watch a parade and Runestone Festival being shot on live television by the "Out There in America" program.

Arrows — or, more specifically, Viking spears carved

of wood by volunteers working under the supervision of the Berryville High School shop teacher — led tourists through the main street of the town toward Sandy Thumb, where the Chamber of Commerce had taken the liberty of fencing off part of a meadow for those who wanted to hear a lecture by a member of the Berryville Archeological Society on the topography of the coast-line in the area where Duane Minnick had found the Berryville Runestone. By midmorning, a line of cars had choked the road on the way to the meadow, and the crowd inside was beginning to strain the temporary fenc-ing. Not more than a hundred yards away, Gerald Baker Manley stood on his porch, peering through his tele-scope for encroachments on his property. He held an electrified megaphone at the ready, in case he had to warn a tourist away from his fencing by quoting the state trespassing act, which he had printed on an index card that was taped to the porch railing for quick refer-ence. Manley's electrified fence had been given an in-creased voltage for the occasion — a fact that was clearly noted on new signs placed on the fence at six-foot intervals.

By eleven in the morning, an hour before the parade was scheduled to start down Main Street, Roy Bouchard was almost sold out of beer and rocks, as well as T-shirts that said "Get Stoned in Berryville." Crowds of tourists were taking pictures of the tractor-gear factory and even the Berryville Free Library — although, to DicCarlo's increasing exasperation, the most popular subject for tourist snapshots turned out to be the information stand attendants dressed in colonial costumes.

"Stupid goddamned tourists," DiCarlo said, as he entered the Yankee Cafe for the fourth time that morning. "They don't know a colonialist from a goddamned Viking and they probably don't know a Viking from a goddamned Canuck. Three of 'em already asked me when the Indian dances are going to start." A number of the town's leading businessmen had agreed to take a few minutes off for a meeting at eleven-fifteen to make certain that the various aspects of the festival were being properly coordinated, and the gathering that resulted was difficult to distinguish from the crowd that regularly assembled at the Yankee Cafe on nonfestival mornings. DiCarlo sat on the edge of the chair that had been reserved for him. "The damn parade is already twenty minutes behind schedule forty-five minutes before it's even scheduled to begin," he said.

"What's the problem?" Henry LaDoux said. "Did you have trouble persuading some of the float drivers that the pothole they've feared since childhood is really gone?"

"No, Myrna McDonald's still getting into her goddamned clothes," DiCarlo said.

"That'll be a change for her," Art Norton said.

"Listen, I gotta go," DiCarlo said, standing up and taking a few quick sips of coffee. "The honorary vice-consul of Finland from Boston is on his way over to the reviewing stand, and if that crazy Swede Gustafson catches him he'll scare him right back to Boston talking all that crap about how the Swedes invented panty hose in the Middle Ages and then we won't have anyone at all in the Diplomatic Corps section. Don't even ask me about the Jaycees and their clams." He raced for the door.

After the mayor left, there was a lull in the conversation. The regulars stirred their coffee and studied the movements of Heather Palermo as she cleared off a table near the front of the cafe. As they stared at Heather, there was an occasional muttered "Boy, what I wouldn't give . . ." or "Jesus, willya look at that," but such mutterings had become so much a part of the coffee-drinkers' staring at Heather that they were taken as background noise rather than conversation — like the sound of spoons on coffee cups. "Lot of excitement," LaDoux finally said. "I'm surprised you're not out writing all this up for the paper, Art."

"We have two of our best spellers on it," Norton said. "Actually, I think I did my part with today's editorial — 'Welcome Visitors.' I don't want to burn myself out."

"Do you think Larry's going to last the day?" Mike Derounian said.

"I wouldn't hazard a guess," Norton said. "If he continues to heat and expand at this rate, we may have to float him, like Mickey Mouse in the Macy's Thanksgiving day parade."

The distinguished visitors waiting at the reviewing stand included the local Congressman, two members of the county executive board, a state Senator, two representatives of the Governor, a juvenile court judge, and the Finnish consul — Martin O'Leary, a Boston import-export man who had been named to the honorary post three years before, after arranging several deals that exchanged Finnish machine lubricants for Costa Rican cocoa to the benefit of both countries and himself. George Gustafson had, as the mayor feared, wandered into the reviewing stand to do some lobbying, but he had cornered the Congressman rather than the Finnish consul. For years, the failure of Congress to set aside a day in honor of Leif Ericson had been used by Gustafson as an example of the historical distortion caused by Italian political influence. "Here we have a day set aside for just about any Southern European mercenary who stumbles across Santo Domingo because he's hopelessly lost," Gustafson was saying to the Congressman. "But for the true discoverer of the country, the man who was able to come straight to these shores because his own people had practically invented the sextant as we know it today, a commander of wooden ships that still serve as models —"

"Very interesting," the Congressman was saying. "Very interesting. Isn't that interesting! How interesting!" The Congressman was peering out of the corner of his eye at the television crew, just in case the producer decided to take up some of the slack time with an interview of some local political personality. The Congressman was not optimistic about his chances of capturing any free air time. The "Out There in America" announcers — a splendidly turned-out couple who seemed to reflect broad smiles in their voices — showed signs of being able to fill as much time as possible talking to each other.

"It's great to be here, isn't it, Kitty?" the male announcer was saying.

"It certainly is, Brad," his partner said, smiling into the camera. "Just great."

"Great," Brad said.

"Great," Kitty said.

"It's great to be here in the American town where it may all have begun, lo so many years ago," Brad said. "Where this whole ballgame of ours may have started."

"It makes you pause," Kitty said.

"But we'll be right back after —"

"No, I don't mean pause for a commercial, Brad," Kitty said. "I mean it makes you pause and think about what it means to be here in this country, where everyone is free to have events just like this."

"It sure does, Kitty, and —"

"But now we do have to pause for a commercial, Brad," Kitty said. "But we'll be back in a minute here at the first annual Berryville Runestone Festival in Berryville, Maine."

Gustafson had withdrawn some photocopies of *Karlsefni's Saga* in the original and was translating them, rather laboriously, for the Congressman, who said it was a very interesting saga. The Finnish consul had just closed a deal for some Argentine horse bristles with the state Senator, who happened to be in the hairbrush business.

"We're going to have a great time out here today, Kitty," Brad said, after the commercial break. "Just one more in a series of events brought to you on 'Out There in America' to give all of you folks out there some idea of what this country is like in all its nooks and crannies, out where people really live."

"Because we really want you people living out there to know how people live, out there," Kitty said.

"And now I see the mayor of Berryville, Lawrence I. DiCarlo, coming into the reviewing stand, Kitty, and I think the parade might just be getting under way."

"It certainly is, Brad. Here's the fire truck with the flashing lights leading the floats, and behind it the first float — a Viking ship with residents of Berryville in Viking dress on it. And on the boat you can see spelled out in clamshells 'Berryville is Vinland.' This lead float is sponsored by Earl's Texaco Station. And every costume, I notice here, Brad, is homemade except for the horns. And every single one of those clamshells — fourteen hundred and fifty-five clamshells — is an actual clamshell."

"It sure is, Kitty," Brad said. "And right behind the Viking float is the Berryville High School Roarin' Redskin Band, under the direction of Frank Manucci, playing the *Arrivederci Roma March*. Look at 'em strut, Kitty."

"Great. And the Indians, of course, Brad, were here in America even before the Vikings arrived here in the Berryville area."

"The first Americans, Kitty. That's right. And they have a lot to teach all of us — respect for the land, for instance, and, uh . . ."

"The water, Brad. Respect for the water."

"Right you are, Kitty. They're a great people. And the next float is . . . well . . ." Pickets had just appeared directly across from the reviewing stand, right in the line of the camera filming the floats. Milly Duffrin was in the lead, holding a placard that said "We Will Not Sell Our Heritage for a Mess of Stones." A dozen members of the Berryville Historical Society marched behind her, carrying signs like "Only Russian Communists Rewrite History" and "DiCarlo is a Traitor to His Race." In order to avoid showing the pickets, the camera had jumped to the fifth or sixth float — skipping, among other entries, the Swedish Historical Institute's float, a huge statue of Leif Ericson under a banner that said "The True Discoverer."

"My God!" said George Gustafson, who had been watching the parade on a monitor to see how the Ericson float would appear to the country at large. "My God! They've done it again!" He pointed to the cameraman. "That man's an Italian," he shouted. "Police chief! I want that man's identity card inspected."

The police chief, Max Hebert, was, as it happened, busy talking to Mayor DiCarlo, who had hurried from the reviewing stand to seek him out the moment the pickets appeared. "Isn't there any way we can arrest them, Max?" the mayor asked.

"C'mon, Larry. You don't pay me enough to try to arrest Milly Duffrin," Hebert said. "She'd chew my ear off about it for the rest of my life. Just relax. They're just going to stand there, and the goddamned tourists will probably think they're part of the show."

DiCarlo returned to the reviewing stand, and tried to ignore the pickets. He saluted when the American Legion color guard went by. He even brought himself to wave and smile at the huge convertible decorated with banners that said "Discoverers of the Berryville Runestone" and carrying Duane Minnick and Clifford Bates. After the "Maxine Thomas Live" incident, DiCarlo had wanted to ban Clifford from the parade, but Duane had refused to participate without him. Both Duane and Clifford were sitting on top of the convertible's back seat, dressed in their best clothes. Duane had on the outfit he had been saving for his first big country and western audition — a bright gold leisure suit, a string tie, and cowboy boots. Clifford was waving cheerfully to the crowd, but Duane, looking pale and nervous, sat frozen except when Clifford's occasional elbow to the ribs would stir him to an awkward half-wave.

"Relax, Duane," Clifford said out of the side of his mouth. "You're a hero. Look at all that scroggin' material out there waving at you, Duane. You discovered the stone, Duane. You're going to be knee-deep in scroggin' material."

"You got the speech, Clifford?" Duane asked for the fourth or fifth time. He was trying to whisper, but his voice sounded as if it might not go above a whisper whether he was trying or not.

"I got it, Duane," Clifford said. "Don't worry. The camera's on you now. Give them that old smile, Duane. Hit them with that old come-and-get-me-girls smile."

Duane managed to approximate a smile as the convertible came into camera range. "There he is, Kitty," Brad said into the microphone. "You see him now, ladies and gentlemen. Duane Minnick, the young man who discovered the Berryville Runestone and brought it in for authentication to Sam Brewster of the Berryville Museum — and all this without one single day of formal archeological training. Isn't that something, Kitty?"

"Great, Brad," Kitty said.

"And with him, his good friend Clifford Bates, the young man who was clamming with Duane Minnick at the time — also with no formal archeological training."

"Yes sir, none at all, Brad."

"Right, Kitty."

Clifford smiled and waved to the crowd. He shouted, "Hi there, visitors!" over and over as he waved, except when the band just behind him was playing loudly enough to drown out the sound of his voice, at which time he alternated "Hi there, visitors" with "Up yours, suckers" — still smiling and waving.

"And coming up, Brad," Kitty said. "The Viking Princess. The first annual Viking Princess in the first of what the folks in Berryville hope will become an event celebrated every year. She is Miss Myrna McDonald of Berryville."

"There she is, Kitty. And maybe you should do the honors in describing her regal array."

"Thanks, Brad. As all of you can see, the Princess is wearing a strapless gold ball-gown, a necklace fashioned by Mrs. Hector Ferrera of Berryville out of local semiprecious stones and clamshells, pumps furnished by La-Doux's Family Fashions of Berryville, and — here's a departure — instead of a crown a beehive hairdo with two horns in it to simulate a Viking motif. Very, very attractive."

"She certainly is, Kitty," Brad said. "And Myrna is the daughter of Mr. and Mrs. Joseph McDonald of Berryville and is a graduate of Berryville High School. Myrna's hobbies are swimming and ecology."

The band between Myrna and the convertible carrying Duane and Clifford broke into the Berryville High School fight song. Myrna waved demurely at the crowd. Duane tried a tight smile and a half-wave. Clifford held his arms aloft, like a victorious politician enveloping the crowd, and smiled, and shouted into the noise of the band, "The Princess does it for quarters" and "She'd hump King Kong for a Mars bar" and "Hi there, visitors."

The parade ended at Berryville City Park, where the bandstand had been decorated and folding chairs arranged for the awards ceremony. Preparations had also been made for the Jaycee clambake that was to follow the speeches. Huge vats of clams stood ready. Police barricades marked out a serving line. Picnic tables had been scattered throughout the park. The Jaycees were anxious to have the ceremony begin — they had begun steaming the clams too early, having been unaware of the delay in the parade — but it had to be held up until the "Out There in America" camera crew had moved its equipment from the reviewing stand to scaffolding that had been erected just to the side of the City Park bandstand. Mayor DiCarlo spent the delay rearranging the seating on the bandstand and complaining about the inability of the Jaycees to complete successfully even a task as simple as steaming clams. "Goddamned young executive future leaders of the world," he muttered to the Finnish consul. "They couldn't find their fly to piss out of."

When the television cameras had been set up, the director gave DiCarlo the signal, and the mayor stepped to the podium. He began by recognizing the dignitaries gathered on the bandstand. Then he drew a speech out of his pocket. "The ways of history are mighty and strange," the mayor said. "Here we are gathered in Berryville. A city of churches. A fine place to live and work. The first city to be called Heart of the Yankee Shore. The third city in the state to have one hundred percent sodium street lighting. A city that, we believe, will someday have the most modern water-treatment plant in the state of Maine. But, for all of that, a humble city. Yes, it happens to have a modern industrial park and an industrial tax incentive program that compares with the finest in the Northeast. Yes, it has a skilled labor force. But, for all that, it is a humble city — a city of just plain friends and neighbors. Who would think that this city, Berryville, our hometown, might be Vinland? And what do you know — that's what it is, Vinland. And we wouldn't have known any of this. We might have gone along thinking we were nothing but the Heart of the Yankee Shore, with the proof of Vinland just a few yards away, except for one of our fine young residents, Duane Minnick. Duane Minnick comes from a family that has been in Berryville for many generations. His brother is serving his country now in the Armed Forces. Duane himself attended our schools and now is one of the fine young men who chose to live in this community — one of our future leaders, you might say. Today, a day that every resident in Berryville has reason to be proud of, the first annual Berryville Runestone Festival, it gives me a great pleasure to present our first Distinguished Viking Award to the person who, along with Leif Ericson, made this all possible — a fine young man, our very own Duane Minnick."

There was enthusiastic applause, except from Milly Duffrin and the other Historical Society pickets, who stood silently in front of the stage, holding up their placards. Duane remained in his seat. Clifford, who was sitting next to Duane on the bandstand, pressed the speech into his hand and began poking him. Finally, Duane stood up, unsteadily, and walked to the podium, clutching the speech in both hands. He began reading it, in a loud, flat voice, as if reading a proclamation. "Your Honor Mayor DiCarlo, honored guests, Viking Princess, friends," he began, stumbling only on the word "honored." He took a deep breath, and continued. "I am proud to be here. I did nothing that any other redblooded American would not have done. I am proud to be a Berryviller. I am proud that Berryville, my home town, is Vinland. I am proud to receive this award. And I am pleased to be able to announce that the words written on the runestone have been translated by a crypt . . . a crypt . . . crypt . . ."

"Cryptographer," Clifford hissed from his seat a few feet away. DiCarlo and John R. Sprigg III exchanged puzzled looks.

"Cryptographer," Duane said, concentrating his entire attention on the piece of paper he was reading. "And, ladies and gentlemen, those words are as follows . . ." The crowd grew silent. John Sprigg stood up and started toward the podium. "Those words are, 'I don't know but I've been told that Eskimo nookie is mighty cold.' "

Milly Duffrin dropped her placard. Mayor DiCarlo fainted — or, as several eyewitnesses put it, "just sputtered out." John R. Sprigg snatched up a folding chair and was restrained by Chief Hebert just before he got close enough to swing it at Duane. Sam Brewster said, "That's certainly more than six words." Clifford Bates collapsed in laughter.

"You O.K., Larry?" Mike Derounian asked. It was the Monday morning after the first annual Berryville Runestone Festival, and DiCarlo had slouched into the Yankee Cafe at eight-thirty, looking uncharacteristically uncombative.

"I can't believe it," DiCarlo said. "I just can't believe it." He sat down at the table usually occupied by the regulars. Heather Palermo came over and stood patiently, order book poised, waiting for his order. "One cup of black coffee, please, Heather," DiCarlo said. Heather wrote down the order, slowly and carefully, and left to get the coffee. Mike Derounian sat down at the table.

"You can't believe what, Larry?" he said.

"I can't believe that with all the laws on the books, all the city ordinances, all the whole goddamned state penal code, there is no way to put that little bastard Clifford Bates in jail."

"Art Norton said Clifford gave the town a hundred thousand dollars' worth of free publicity," Derounian said.

"That doesn't mean he should be roaming the streets," DiCarlo said. Heather brought the coffee, and DiCarlo stirred it listlessly. "It's getting so Max Hebert won't arrest anybody," he went on. "He wouldn't arrest Milly Duffrin. He wouldn't arrest that little pissant Duane Minnick. He won't arrest Clifford Bates. It's freedom hall around here for the criminal element."

A few of the regulars — Henry LaDoux, John Houghton, Art Norton, Vinnie Marchetti — came into the Yankee Cafe and sat down. They all greeted the mayor with some solicitousness. "That street where the pothole was looks real good now, Larry," LaDoux said. "You can be proud of that job. Never know a pothole had ever been there." DiCarlo said nothing.

"We were just saying the same thing on the way over," Houghton said. "Smooth as could be."

"It was embarrassing up there for a public official," DiCarlo said. "I mean, in front of the Finnish consul and all."

"I think you handled it very well, Larry," Derounian said.

"Absolutely," Houghton said. "They always tell us at the head office that the best thing to do in a case like that is to say absolutely nothing."

"That is certainly one of the advantages of losing consciousness," Art Norton said. "It prevents someone from saying something he may later regret."

"And look at all the publicity, Larry," Derounian said. "For just a minute or two of embarrassment, it was worth it. Didn't *Time* call up the paper to ask about a story, Art?"

"I believe both *Time* and *Newsweek* may have stories in their Press sections this week," Norton said. "Apparently, one toilet-tongue catching both Maxine Thomas and the 'Out There in America' smilers within the same week is considered a record. The fellow from *Time* particularly enjoyed Brad and Kitty's reaction — Brad breaking down in tears and Kitty saying, 'Shit, shit, shit, shit, shit.' I'll have to admit that I rather enjoyed it myself."

"Johnny-Three says Fornus Mitchell's really excited about the whole thing, Larry," LaDoux said.

DiCarlo grunted.

"Who's Fornus Mitchell?" Houghton asked.

"He's the guy Johnny-Three talked to about the theme-park," LaDoux said. "He told Johnny-Three that with all this publicity the theme-park is bound to be a gold mine even if the rock turns out to have been made in Hong Kong. It's going to be great, Larry. Larry?"

DiCarlo shifted slightly in his chair. "I don't know," he said. "Maybe. We'll probably never be able to get hold of the land anyway. If we ever figure out who owns it, somebody like Manley will have grabbed it already."

"I'm afraid you haven't heard the latest chapter of the saga, Your Honor," Art Norton said.

"Have you been holding out news on us again, Art?" Derounian said.

"I only hold out news on the readers," Norton said. "I always tell you sooner or later. I just like to wait for an appropriate lull in the conversation."

"Well, what is it?" LaDoux said.

"I just happen to have a copy here of a letter Johnny-

Three received this morning in his role as chairman of the Economic Development Commission," Norton said. He withdrew a piece of paper from his jacket. "I'll do my best to read it," he went on. "And if I stumble occasionally I'm sure you gentlemen will know to attribute it to the difficulty of reading a copy made on the copying machine the aforementioned economic developer provides for his staff. It begins, after addressing itself to Johnny-Three by his appropriate civic title and to his appropriate address, 'Dear Mr. Sprigg. It has come to my attention that the Berryville Economic Development Commission, of which you are chairman (as well as chairman of the Acquisitions Subcommittee), has been making inquiries as to the ownership of the thirty acres of land commonly known as Sandy Thumb. This letter is to inform you that I am the sole owner of the property in question and have a clear deed to same in my possession. I have reason to believe that there might be other prospective buyers for this parcel of land in the area. However, as a resident of Berryville interested in furthering the economic development of the city, I would certainly be agreeable to entertaining offers from your committee before seeking counteroffers elsewhere. I shall look forward to hearing from you on this matter at your earliest convenience. With best personal wishes, I remain yours sincerely, John Ronald Sprigg IV.'"

Mayor DiCarlo regained his energy. "Ronnie Sprigg!"

153

he shouted, coming out of his chair. "Ronnie Sprigg! That little pantywaist bastard! It's a conspiracy! It's obviously a goddamned conspiracy cooked up by Ronnie Sprigg! I can't believe it! It's obvious! It's unbelievable! It's as plain as the nose on your goddamned face! Jesus Christ!"

"Take it easy, Larry," Derounian said. "We don't know that it's a conspiracy. Maybe Ronnie heard both the committee and Manley were after the land so he figured out how to get there first."

"Maybe he did it just to piss off his father," LaDoux said. "Everybody wants to piss off his father these days."

"He's always been so polite, the little backstabber," DiCarlo said. "He'd say 'excuse me' if a truck ran over him, the little fruitcake bastard."

"I'd say addressing your own father as 'Mr. Sprigg' in formal correspondence qualifies as being on a high level of courtesy," Norton said. "It was also rather courteous of him, I think, to include best personal wishes."

The door opened suddenly, and Jeffrey Bryant burst into the Yankee Cafe. He glanced around the restaurant for a moment, and then, spotting Norton, he hurried over to the table. "I found it, Mr. Norton," he said. "I've got the goods on him." Bryant was obviously too excited to worry about reporting in front of the others at the table. "It was our own publisher after all, Mr. Norton. I just got it all figured out at the deeds office. One person has put together all the land of Sandy Thumb, and that person, right on the deeds, is none other than J. R. Sprigg!"

"It's a shame we can't print that," Norton said. "It happens to be the one name we can always spell."

"The roast squab is marvelous, Mr. Jones — one of your triumphs." Ronnie Sprigg was in his customary booth in Wong's Garden of the Orient, passing some time with Alonzo Jones while eating some roast squab and a side dish of stuffed bean curd with brown sauce.

"You're very kind, Mr. Sprigg," Jones said. "With so many of my patrons laboring under the belief that shrimp chow mein is the most exotic dish Western man was meant to consume, I have few enough opportunities to prepare food for someone with a sophisticated palate such as your own."

"A triumph," Sprigg repeated, finishing off the last of the stuffed bean curd.

"I take it that your letter to your father regarding the Sandy Thumb matter caused quite a stir among the business leaders of Berryville," Jones said.

"I understand that it did, Mr. Jones. Although I thought it was an open and straightforward way to begin a real estate negotiation."

"Businessmen in the retail trades do tend to be suspicious," Jones said. "I believe it was a French writer who said, 'The petite bourgeoisie fear the tax-collector and each other.' I suppose they inferred from your letter that because you had put together the parcel for sale you must have had something to do with the discovery that made it so valuable."

"I wouldn't be at all surprised if they did make that inference, Mr. Jones," Sprigg said.

"And I suppose they think you are now planning to hold them up with the threat that you might sell the land to Gerald Baker Manley," Jones said.

"I suspect their thinking might go along that line," Sprigg said.

Sprigg and Jones sat silently for a while. Sprigg, finding a bit of sauce left in the dish that had held the bean curd, poured it over the few grains that remained in his rice bowl and began eating again. Jones watched him approvingly. "Would you say, Mr. Sprigg," Jones said, "that the conflict between the summer people and the Main Street merchants is a conflict between the landed middle class and the entrepreneurial middle class?"

"That's an interesting distinction, as all of yours always are, Mr. Jones," Sprigg said. "Class, of course, has been notoriously difficult to measure objectively in this country."

"Did I ever tell you my cousin's experience in that field, Mr. Sprigg?"

"You mean the cousin who was a chef in the Rumanian-Jewish restaurant?"

"Yes, that cousin," Jones said. "He had to quit the Rumanian-Jewish restaurant because of persistent heartburn, strange as that may sound. He couldn't seem to resist sampling what he cooked, and the reaction of his body amounted to what he always called 'genetic rejection.' He became a statistician for a social scientist who believed that the class of a club or a neighborhood in the United States could be placed precisely by taking waist and thigh measurements of the women between the ages of thirty-five to forty-five. The theory, of course, was that interest in personal appearance and opportunities to exercise and knowledge of healthy and slenderizing diets increased with class, so that class could be measured exactly in inverse proportion to the average waist and thigh measurements."

"How interesting," Sprigg said. "What were the results of the study, Mr. Jones?"

"Unfortunately, they were never compiled," Jones said. "It turned out that what interested the social scientist was not the results but the opportunity to measure thighs. Waists held no particular interest for him. There was a small scandal, which does not, of course, invalidate the theory."

"Fascinating, Mr. Jones," Sprigg said.

"On the other hand," Jones said. "One way to interpret the attitude of the summer people is as a desire to live in a world that does not have a middle class. Aesthetically,

Manley would have no objection to a mansion being built on Sandy Thumb or to a tumbling fisherman's shack. But to avoid looking out on a sanitary and efficiently run but exceedingly middle-class theme-park, he would probably give a hundred thousand dollars."

"An interesting theory, Mr. Jones," Sprigg said. "Although I was thinking more in terms of two hundred thousand."

"But if your own son owns the land, I don't see the problem, Mr. Sprigg," Fornus Mitchell said. Mitchell had just arrived in Berryville; he and John R. Sprigg III were holding their first meeting in Sprigg's office at the newspaper. A short, natty man, Mitchell was dressed in vaguely Western style — a carefully cut white suit, a string tie, cowboy boots, and a wide-brimmed hat. He spoke in rapid bursts of words. He had brought with him a portfolio of oversized artist's renderings of the proposed Viking Village, along with plans and photographs of other family theme-parks he had designed. Mitchell stood in front of the windowsill, where he had propped up the Viking Village drawings. Sprigg paced slowly up and down the length of his office.

"My son has always been rather independent," Sprigg said.

"Generational revolt," Mitchell said. "Nature's way. They're all like that. Rebels against authority. I wanted to do a theme-park on it once. Let it all hang out. Wax museum with tableaux of all the worst parents in history. A big Lizzie Borden outdoor drama. Split screen cyclorama showing ROTC buildings being burned down. All that."

"That's not quite the problem, Mr. Mitchell," Sprigg said. Ronnie's attitude toward the traditions and professions of the John R. Spriggs who had preceded him could not really be called rebellious; he simply seemed disinclined to participate. Ronnie's behavior, in fact, had always had an eerie sort of perfection to it — like the behavior of a cadet who is exceedingly careful about avoiding demerits. He had never spoken disrespectfully to his father. He always cleaned up his room without being told. No rebel had ever been that courteous. But Ronnie had always kept his distance. Sprigg had no idea how to approach his son about the subject of the Sandy Thumb land; he had, to his distress, even considered answering Ronnie's formal business letter with a formal business letter of his own.

"John," Fornus Mitchell was saying. "I can call you John — O.K.? Or Jack? No, John. John, this is a gold mine. A gold mine. We're talking about a gold mine. A natural. Sure, maybe we'd be better off with the rock to display. But this way we've got the mystery of its disappearance. Adds to the whole atmosphere. Look, I've got this sculptor working on a dinosaur park in Nebraska now. Prestressed concrete dinosaurs. A tyrannosaurus fifty-four feet high. Fabulous stuff. Fabulous. I can get him right after the dinosaurs are done. He can do Viking ships. It's the same principal. And John, the gift shops in this one are a natural — all that wooden junk from Norway and Denmark. A natural! It's a gold mine, John."

"The Acquisitions Subcommittee will be having a meeting about the land," Sprigg said. He had always made all of the decisions for the Acquisitions Subcommittee without the formality of a meeting — not to speak of all the decisions for the Economic Development Commission and even most of the decisions for the executive board of the Chamber of Commerce. But, for the first time, he felt a strong need to depend on somebody else's decision-making.

"Norwegian ski sweaters. Swedish ski sweaters. Ski sweaters," Mitchell went on. "It's a natural, John. We'll have to build a pond, of course. For the Viking ships. Fill in the tidal pond. Saltwater could gum up the works if we have anything mechanical popping in and out, like sea monsters."

"The land simply may be priced out of our range," Sprigg said. He had no idea what price Ronnie had in mind. He had hardly permitted himself to think of the possibility that Ronnie had concocted the runestone to enhance the value of the land. Why? To prove his independence? To make a fool out of his own father?

"Beer," Mitchell said. "Scandinavian beer. Tuborg. Carlsberg. A natural, John, a natural. Those Scandinavian beer companies are going to eat this up."

When the summer people gathered that Saturday evening at Gerald Baker Manley's house, there was no pretext of a casual evening together. They had come to talk about the threat to Sandy Thumb. Schmule and Leah Rifkind arrived first — having obviously discussed the matter beforehand between themselves, since Schmule began talking about it as the Manleys greeted him. "A rabbi in Vitebsk once had something to say on this subject," he told Manley. "A half-crazed Hasidic rabbi, as it happens, but so many of them possessed almost magical wisdom, the way some idiot savants possess seemingly magical powers to multiply multidigit numbers. At any rate, this rabbi wrote that a man who never owns land is forever a tenant. It appears to be something of a truism, now that I think of it, but at least it doesn't sound as if it might have been said by a Cheyenne medicine man."

"There's great insight there, Schmule," Manley said. "I often tell Blake here how lucky we are to have a world-class intellectual in our little community."

"What?" Rifkind said, turning to Leah.

Leah just tapped her temple a couple of times with

her forefinger, having long ago reduced all compliments on her husband's intellect to a simple gesture.

Porter Fox, the left-wing writer, also arrived early, in order to have a few minutes to talk with the Manleys about a fund-raising campaign for an imprisoned Paraguayan intellectual. Fox and Consuela López de la Riviera had split up, but Fox had brought along a Belgian countess he had encountered while working on a series of articles about continuing European economic imperialism in the former French colonies of West Africa. Richard and Andrea Fenton were there, and so were Dominick Searle and Earl Sawyer, who had, after two months apart, effécted an emotional reconciliation that everyone in the summer colony said was the best thing for both of them, as well as a reaffirmation of the deep relationships that really could be formed in alternate life-styles.

As Manley began a discussion of the Berryville Runestone and its impact on the summer community, he noticed that the attempts at phrasemaking normally heard when the summer people discussed any subject — Broadway plays or baseball or real estate or household detergents — seemed to be missing. It occurred to him that a number of his guests were willing to discuss the runestone only in a rather guarded way, as if protecting a few of their most highly polished observations for future publication. Richard Fenton had, in fact, mentioned doing an article on the land-use and zoning implications of the discovery for a legal quarterly that enjoyed wide readership among laymen. It was assumed by everyone that Porter Fox would eventually write about the runestone in economic terms — as a reflection of American consumerism and its implications. Manley knew from his contacts in the world of scholarly journals that Schmule Rifkind had been asked to set down the thoughts the runestone inspired in him for an intellectual quarterly called *Per Se, A Journal of Meaningful Dialogue*. Manley was pleased at the lack of witticisms. He planned to handle the situation as a straightforward business matter.

"I've managed to learn, through a clerk in the deeds office, that the Sandy Thumb parcel is owned by one person and is for sale," Manley said. "It is owned by Ronnie Sprigg, the son of John R. Sprigg III, a man many of you have probably met here. Although Ronnie has apparently expressed a preference for selling the land to the town for development as a theme-park, there is every reason to believe a higher offer may prevail."

"But doesn't that mean he cooked up the whole thing?" Andrea Fenton asked. "He must have just put together the plot of land and then planted a fake stone to make the land more valuable."

"Perhaps," Manley said. "Although that means he somehow got Duane Minnick to discover the stone and that he arranged to have Clifford Bates get a picture and that he managed to have the stone lost and that he knows enough about Old Norse to fool eminent scholars of the subject and that he knows enough about codes to befuddle the CIA or wherever the mayor has arranged to have the code studied by professional cryptographers. And even if all of that is true, which seems to me unlikely, it would, in my judgment, be impossible to prove."

"What?" Rifkind said to Leah.

"Some *shegetz* owns the land," Leah said in her husband's ear.

"But why would we have to prove it?" Richard Fenton asked Manley. "If we can just cast enough suspicion on this kid to make everybody think the rock is probably a fake, then Berryville isn't Vinland, so the town won't be bidding against us to get the land for a theme-park and we can save the land for, well, future generations and the ecological cycle."

"If we smear the *shegetz,* we get the land cheap," Leah shouted at her husband, without waiting to be asked.

"Unfortunately, Dick, that might not be the case," Manley said. "Some of you have much more experience in the communications field than I do, but the people I've asked about this seem to think that an attempt to expose Sprigg might cause a backlash. A psychologist at Harvard who specializes in this sort of thing told me

that, in the first place, people are likely to want to believe that Berryville is Vinland — it's both romantic and
concrete — and could resent any efforts to undermine
that belief. Also, the suspicion of a fantastic hoax might
make Berryville more famous as the setting for the hoax
than it would have been as Vinland. Apparently, the
fellow at Harvard tells me, Ronnie Sprigg could become
a national hero — like the man who got away with the
airplane hijacking on the West Coast and became a great
hero, with people wearing T-shirts with his picture on
them. We can't be certain of that, of course, but I think
we'd be much safer to meet his terms."

"What?" Schmule Rifkind said.

"He wants to pay off the *shegetz*," Leah told him.

Dominick Searle stood up. "Gerry," he said. "This boy
might want a hundred thousand dollars for that land,
now that two factions are fighting over it."

"I figure more like two hundred thousand would be
necessary to take it," Manley said. At least three people
in the room groaned. Leah Rifkind held up two fingers
for her husband to see.

"Gerry," Dominick Searle said. "I think you'll have to
face the fact that we'd have trouble getting that kind of
money together, speaking for our own household at
least. After all, all we'd be getting for the money was
protection; we wouldn't want to use the property."

"Actually, we're pretty sure it wouldn't cost any of us

anything," Manley said. He gestured toward John Kaye, one of the Harvard Law School professors. "I've asked John to look into the tax picture on this, since tax is his field, and he's come up with some interesting findings. John . . ."

"What?" Rifkind said, as John Kaye stood up. "What's he saying?"

"The basic strategy is to form a corporation that later becomes a foundation, unless the numbers come out better the other way around," Kaye said. "The corporation or foundation buys the land, using a collateral-free loan available to trusts operating in this state under circumstances rather too complicated to explain without boring everyone. At any rate, the trust then donates the land, probably to the nature conservancy or some outfit like that, taking a loss and/or charitable contribution write-off for that, depending on which way we decide to depreciate it. I think, depending on your tax bracket, we could safely say that each person involved will make about two percent on his money the first year — that is on paper, of course; in practice, you will not have put up any actual money — and have a write-off of several thousand dollars in each of the ensuing fifteen years. And, of course, we'd have the land protected in perpetuity."

"What'd he say?" Schmule shouted.

"If we grab the land," Leah shouted back, "the government pays."

Most of the regulars were assembled at their usual table in the Yankee Cafe when Sam Brewster walked in. It was almost nine in the morning, on the Monday after the summer colony had met at Gerald Baker Manley's house to discuss the purchase of Sandy Thumb. Brewster walked straight back to the table and, without sitting down, said, formally, "Gentlemen, it is my sad duty to inform you that Berryville is not Vinland after all."

There was a long silence. Sam Brewster sat down. "Well," Roy Bouchard said. "I'm glad at least about the pothole."

"I knew it," Mayor DiCarlo said. "I said right away that little pissant Duane Minnick couldn't find his way out of bed in the morning. I knew that fruitcake Ronnie Sprigg cooked this whole thing up. I knew it."

"Not Ronnie Sprigg," Brewster said.

"What!" DiCarlo said. "What are you talking about? Don't try to protect that sneaky little fairy."

"I think Mike better come back and sit down for what I'm about to say," Brewster said. Heather Palermo having called in sick again, Derounian was busy at the counter, but when DiCarlo motioned to him he came back and joined the regulars. "Mike, we've been friends for a long time," Brewster said to him.

"If you're about to tell him you found something you shouldn't have in the soup yesterday," Art Norton said, "I want you to know that he can explain the presence of practically anything short of earrings in there as part of an old Armenian recipe."

"Yesterday, I finally thought of asking Duane Minnick how he happened to be clamming just where he was clamming — right near that boulder off of Sandy Thumb," Brewster went on. "And he said a customer at Earl's told him that was a great clamming spot. So I asked him if he remembered who the customer was. The customer was Mike Derounian."

Derounian looked stunned.

"As I remember the way these things go now," Norton said, "you're supposed to run for the front door, Mike. Then Sam is supposed to tackle you, and you're supposed to confess all. You might as well confess what you put in the soup as long as you're at it."

"Jesus Christ," Derounian said, shaking his head. "I forgot that I told him that. But he's right. I did tell him. I stopped in for some gas, and he said he was going clamming, and I said I heard it was good clamming near that boulder. I remember, because Heather had told me about it . . . Jesus Christ! Heather?"

"My God!" Roy Bouchard said. "Me, too. She told me, too. I never thought of it until just now. I ordered clam chowder one day and she said that speaking of clams

168

there were supposed to be buckets of them down at the end of Sandy Thumb. I should have remembered it, because that's about the only time she ever said anything to me at all except that time she asked me how to spell soup."

"Me, too," Henry LaDoux said. "She told me that, and I didn't even have to order clam chowder. Franks and beans, I think it was."

"That's it!" DiCarlo said, leaping from his chair. "It's Heather!"

"But how could it be Heather?" LaDoux asked. "Heather couldn't think up a stunt like that. Half the time, she can't even think up what to answer when you say Good Morning."

"Not Heather. Her boyfriend," DiCarlo said. "All we have to do is find the sneaky bastard Heather's been spending her time with and that's the one who told her to tip Mike to the boulder and that's the son of a bitch I'm going to arrest myself if Max Hebert won't do it. Conspiracy to defraud. Forgery. Disturbing the peace. Lascivious carriage. Some goddamned thing." DiCarlo turned toward the door. He looked as if his method for catching the culprit might be to run up and down the streets of Berryville until the prey was flushed out and cornered.

"Sit down for a minute, Larry," Roy Bouchard said.

The mayor sat down. "Who else knows about this, Sam?" Bouchard asked Brewster.

"Nobody, except Duane himself, of course," Brewster said.

"Well, why does anybody else have to know?" Bouchard said. "Why not let him get away with it? Why not just go ahead and float some bonds and try to get the land from Ronnie and start the theme-park?"

"I thought you were against the bonds and this whole thing, Roy," Henry LaDoux said.

"I was against it until I sold fifteen gross of souvenir rocks on the day of the Runestone Festival," Bouchard said. "Now I'm for it. The Bouchards may have been nothing but French-Canadian farmers, but they have always been able to count."

"But we can't keep this a secret," Sam Brewster said.

"Why not?" Bouchard asked. "The experts can't show the stone is a fake, so how can you be so sure it is? What if all this stuff about good clamming around the boulder is a coincidence. Or, even if it isn't, how do you know that Heather's boyfriend didn't plant a real runestone near that boulder — a stone he found a few miles down the coast, maybe — so his own town could be Vinland?"

"But there's a matter of historical integrity," Brewster said, straightening up in his chair.

"But you told us yourself that the historians agree the Vikings were in North America first anyway," Henry

LaDoux said. "This wouldn't be implying anything that isn't historical fact."

"Absolutely right," Bouchard said. "If people would rather think a stone proves something that doesn't need a stone to prove it, why not let them have the stone? It makes them happy."

"But as a matter of historical fact . . . ," Brewster said.

"Look, Sam," Derounian said. "The meatloaf I serve here on Thursdays is fine. It isn't going to make you sick. It's O.K. But if I told you all the stuff we put in it, you might not want to order it. What I do is not trouble you with the details. This is exactly the same principle."

"I just don't know," Brewster said. "There's the matter of Duane Minnick knowing about this, for instance."

"Duane Minnick!" DiCarlo shouted. "We could pay off that little thug with a guitar pick and a couple of hub-caps."

"Well, I wouldn't want to be engaged in anything like a payoff," Brewster said.

"Sam, you wouldn't even know about it," Bouchard said.

"I just don't know," Brewster said. "As you gentlemen are aware, in matters of historical discourse —"

"Sam," Derounian broke in.

"— the matter of accuracy and full disclosure is most —"

"Sam," Derounian repeated.

"Yes?"

"Sam, let's face it," Derounian said. "If this thing comes out as a phony, Milly Duffrin is going to say, 'I told you so' to you for the rest of your life, and I figure she's going to spend about two hours every day saying it."

There was a long silence. "Well, as you say," Brewster finally said, "it's not as if the stone implied an exploration that scholars did not agree existed."

"Mike," Larry DiCarlo said to Derounian, "I'm going to fix your roof."

"I would venture to say that getting both the roof and the pothole fixed makes the discovery of North America seem almost incidental," Norton said.

"I gotta go," DiCarlo said, rising again. "It's all settled, then. We deal with Ronnie Sprigg and forget about Heather's boyfriend."

"You're assuming, Your Honor, that Ronnie Sprigg and Heather's boyfriend could not be the same young American male," Art Norton said.

Everyone at the table laughed. "If Heather was calling in sick to go bird-watching with Ronnie Sprigg, she really *was* sick," Derounian said.

"I want to get my clothes on now, Ron-Ron," Heather Palermo said. She and Ronnie Sprigg were lying on the grass in the hidden clearing he favored for bird-watching —the clearing from which he had watched Duane Minnick pick up the Berryville Runestone.

"Certainly, Heather, if you wish," Ronnie said. "Actually, this may be a good opportunity for us to have a little chat. There's something I've been wanting to tell you."

"I know, Ron-Ron," Heather said, pulling her waitress uniform over her head.

"I'm expecting to come into quite a sum of money soon, Heather."

"I know, Ron-Ron. From Sandy Thumb. Some men at the cafe said you did it to spite your father."

"Oh, goodness no," Ronnie said. "My father has always been very kind to me. I simply thought it would be a prudent investment." Heather nodded silently. "We've often talked about going off somewhere together someday," Ronnie went on. "I believe this would be an appropriate time to do so. The Kingdom of Tonga, in the South Pacific, is the spot I have in mind, although, of course, I'd be pleased to hear any suggestions you have."

"I can never see you again, Ron-Ron," Heather said.

"I beg your pardon?"

"I know that Sandy Thumb is valuable because you tricked me into making someone discover the stone you had planted there. You tricked me into betraying Columbus."

"Who?" Ronnie said.

"Christopher Columbus," Heather said. "Christopher Columbus discovered America, in 1492. He was an Italian. And so am I."

"But he didn't really discover America, Heather," Ronnie said. "Although I think it's awfully nice that you think so. Who was here first really isn't terribly important, but all scholars really do believe the Vikings were here first, runestone or no runestone."

"All scholars are Yankee liars, then," Heather said. "They'd do anything to put down Italians."

"Heather, please, I can assure you I didn't betray Columbus," Ronnie said. "You know I wouldn't do anything like that. I didn't invent the stone. I promise you. I only put it near the boulder. I believe the stone is probably real. I only put it near the boulder because I thought it might as well create a sound investment opportunity as long as it was being discovered anyway. I found it near where Mr. DiCarlo, that nice Italian mayor, has always wanted to put a new water-treatment plant. I couldn't spoil that for him, could I?"

"We were here first," Heather said. "Also, we built the Sistine Chapel and many other important edifices."

"Important edifices? Heather, you haven't been reading books, have you?"

"I have been attending ethnic consciousness-raising sessions given by Professor Vincent Lucelli. He is merely one of many famous scholars who are of Italian descent."

"I can't believe my ears, Heather."

"Vincent said you would react this way," Heather said. "Vincent is a very sophisticated man. Also quite continental."

After an exceedingly polite family dinner during which the subject of the Sandy Thumb land did not come up, John R. Sprigg III had decided that any negotiations with Ronnie about the land should be handled by Fornus Mitchell in order to avoid any appearance of conflict of interest. Mitchell found Ronnie Sprigg courteous and agreeable and enthusiastic about selling the land to the Acquisitions Subcommittee as long as it matched the price offered by the summer people. "I think it would please Father," Ronnie told Mitchell. On the morning after his meeting with Ronnie Sprigg, Mitchell was brought to the Yankee Cafe by John R. Sprigg III to meet the mayor and other interested businessmen — transforming the morning coffee gathering into a more or less official occasion. There were already a dozen men in the back of the Yankee Cafe when Art Norton came in, a few minutes later than usual, nodded to John R. Sprigg III, took a seat, and announced that Duane Minnick had long ago put the stone back where he found it.

Larry DiCarlo, to everyone's surprise, did not begin

shouting or pounding the table. In fact, he spoke softly and slowly — more softly and slowly than anyone had ever heard him speak. "I wonder if I could trouble you to repeat that, Art," he said to Norton.

"I'd be happy to, Your Honor," Norton said. "Young Duane, feeling pangs of a conscience undoubtedly nurtured in him during childhood by the clergymen and scoutmasters of this city, followed up his little chat with Sam by coming into the paper last night and making a confession to me. He confessed that he had, after all, taken the stone from the library after showing it to Sam, that a voice on the telephone that very evening said that hiding the stone in a very safe place until autumn would result in a new set of wide-track radials, and that, acting on the advice of his trusted if highly pornographic friend, Clifford Bates, he took the stone to Sandy Thumb and put it back where it came from."

Everyone at the table looked at DiCarlo. He sat silently for a few moments. "Jesus! What are we waiting for!" he shouted suddenly. "Let's get out there and find the goddamned stone!" He leaped from his chair and ran for his pickup.

At Sandy Thumb, he paused only long enough to leave his shoes on the shore and roll his trousers up a few turns before dashing into the water. Once in the vicinity of the boulder, he rolled up his right shirtsleeve and began reaching down in the water, examining each rock he pulled out, and then tossing it out to sea. "What makes you think this is low tide?" he shouted — to no one in particular, since none of the other businessmen, all similarly occupied examining stones, had suggested it was low tide. "We'll never find it," DiCarlo went on. "This is what those meatheads call a safe place! The surf could have rolled the thing to goddamn China by now, for Christ's sake."

"I hope so," Roy Bouchard said.

"What do you mean — you hope so?" DiCarlo shouted, inspecting three rocks as he spoke, and flinging them away.

"Well, if the thing is a phony, we obviously don't want anybody looking at it closely," Bouchard said.

"Precisely," Fornus Mitchell shouted. "He's right. The man knows." Mitchell was standing in the water not far away from the others, but, instead of inspecting rocks, he was gazing around, trying to ascertain the best place in the area for a concrete Viking ship. "He's right," Mitchell continued. "Even if it's legitimate, finding it would lose the mystery. The mystery is it. Fabulous. Buried treasure. Mysterious disappearance. And now, weird reburial. Fabulous!"

"You mean we should tell everyone that little pissant Duane Minnick reburied the stone?" DiCarlo asked Mitchell.

"Naturally," Mitchell said. "Think of it: millions of stones here and one of them is the greatest artifact in the history of the Western Hemisphere. Needle in the haystack. He'll say he put it back because it belonged to the sea. Very romantic."

"Duane Minnick can't even pronounce romantic," DiCarlo said. "How are we going to bribe him to say something like that?"

"Maybe we can get him a whole car instead of just a set of hubcaps," Bouchard said.

"I've been thinking we might need the car to shut up Clifford Bates," Derounian said. They were now all gathered together, knee deep in the water off Sandy Thumb, discussing the situation as if they were still sitting behind coffee cups at the Yankee Cafe.

"I suspect Clifford could be taken care of if you managed to customize a hardtop with a wide repertoire of obscene noises," Art Norton said.

"And we'll get Duane an audition with a country music producer or something like that," Derounian said.

"Great!" DiCarlo said. "That's it. Maybe we can get him an audition in Nashville and the little pissant will get lost on the way back."

In its fourth week of operation, Viking Village World was considered by Fornus Mitchell to be "in the air and climbing." Attendance was running six percent above even the estimates projected by DiCarlo in the grant application he had filed for some Small Business Administration funds to supplement the Viking Bond Issue —

estimates that themselves had been characterized by Art Norton, though not in print, as "the most imaginative act of DiCarlo's career in public office." Picketing by Milly Duffrin and some other members of the Berryville Historical Society on opening day had only fueled the publicity created by the discovery and the disappearance and the live-television embarrassments and the news of the reburial. Newspapers all over the country had carried a picture of Milly Duffrin, dressed in an authentic colonial gown, walking in front of Viking Village World with a placard that said, "The Rocks Are In Your Head, DiCarlo."

George Gustafson's publishing company, a subsidiary of his beer distributing company, had collaborated with the George Gustafson Foundation on a display called "Viking Culture Through The Ages — From Leif Ericson to Victor Borge." Gustafson was often there himself, handing out fact sheets on runestones in Oklahoma and Montana, or autographing copies of his book on the Berryville Runestone, or lecturing on how the Swedes invented what amounted to the modern piston engine in the fifteenth century. Neither the picketing nor the violence feared from the Italian-American Historical Preservation Society had materialized. Vincent Lucelli, having unexpectedly accepted a chair in navigational history at a university in the Canary Islands, had left Berryville in the company of Heather Palermo.

The theme-park was swarming with people even on weekdays. The dinosaurs-in-cement sculptor had been tracked down by Fornus Mitchell, and an entire armada of Viking ships appeared to sail on the pond that was built after an inlet of Sandy Thumb had been filled in. Within each boat, connected by gangplanks, were shops selling Scandinavian sweaters and dolls and kitchenware. One boat sold only Viking hats, with the buyer's name embroidered across them. Another sold Leif Ericson T-shirts. In the amusement section of the park, there were Viking-boat bumper cars and a Viking-boat ferris wheel; visitors were pulled on Viking boats through tunnels filled with horrifying sea monsters and icebergs. Near the theme-park entrance, an expert on "participatory tourism," a man with experience in several folk-life festivals, had established a "Help Build a Viking Ship" project, in which a visitor could hammer a board into place or help pull up a mast on a Viking ship that would one day be placed in front of the George Gustafson Library and Archive of Scandinavian Discovery in Iowa. A bronze plaque on the ship said, "An authentic replica of the Viking ship that discovered America. Built by those who followed. Berryville, Maine. Vinland." In an effort to maintain a consistent and appropriate decor for the theme-park, all of the signs were done in printing designed to suggest Viking runes. It was often said in the Yankee Cafe that the only garish signs visible to a visitor in the theme-park were those on Gerald Baker Manley's fence — warning trespassers of the legal penalty and painful shock they faced if they dared an incursion.

The main attraction on the beach next to Manley's property was the Personal Archeology Project. A visitor was permitted to wade into the area where Duane Minnick had been standing when the stone was discovered, and, as the brochure for Viking Village World put it, to "take a chance on getting your name in the history books forever as the rediscoverer of the most important historical artifact in the history of the United States." Failure to rediscover the stone did not mean that a participant in the Personal Archeology Project went home empty-handed. As part of the theme-park admission, a visitor had the right to keep one stone found in the water off Sandy Thumb and have it stamped with the official stamp — "This is an official stone from Sandy Thumb, Berryville, Maine, discovered in the Personal Archeology Project to help scientists rediscover the Berryville Rune-stone. (Signed) Lawrence I. DiCarlo, Mayor."

A fortunate visitor might also have his stone autographed by Duane Minnick himself. The contract Duane had finally signed with the theme-park, after considerable negotiation, called for him to be — "permitted him to be" was the actual language — in the theme-park bandstand for two hours each day, singing songs of his own composition over a public address system that carried to every corner of the park. "I have sailed all over, from sea to shining sea," Duane would sing. "But all them castles and native girls don't mean a thing to me. / I can't seem to sail no place that's really to my liking. / You've made me a sad and lonely, broken-hearted, all tore up, little ol' Country Viking. Thwack. Thwack."